CW00432677

Bethou, the tiny Channel island that
had been Philippa's family home for so
long, meant a great deal to her—
especially now that she was trying to
break away from Kevin. But the forceful
Zane Kendrick seemed to think he had a
claim on it too, and he was prepared to
go to some considerable lengths to get
it. Including marrying her . . .

# QUEEN OF
# THE CASTLE

BY

## NICOLA WEST

**MILLS & BOON LIMITED**
15–16 BROOK'S MEWS
LONDON W1A 1DR

*First published 1984*
*Australian copyright 1984*
*Philippine copyright 1984*
*This edition 1984*

© Nicola West 1984

ISBN 0 263 74554 6

*Set in Monophoto Times 10 pt.*
*01–0384 – 67962*

*Made and printed in Great Britain by*
*Richard Clay (The Chaucer Press) Ltd,*
*Bungay, Suffolk*

# CHAPTER ONE

PHILIPPA Ozanne slipped thankfully into the rather hard, single berth and wriggled herself comfortable. She was glad she had booked herself a berth, and she had been doubly thankful when she had arrived on board and seen just how crowded the Channel Islands ferry was. Most of the cabins would certainly have been booked beforehand, with little chance of acquiring one on embarking, and she didn't fancy a night in the crowded lounge, trying to sleep in an upright aircraft-style seat surrounded by other passengers.

Not that she expected to sleep a lot anyway, she reflected as she pulled the dark green blankets up to her chin and switched off the light. There was too much to think about. Like her home on the tiny island of Bethou, just off Guernsey. Whether she was going to stay there after her father's funeral, make her life there, or sell the house and island and return to the mainland. That was something she wouldn't know until she actually saw it again. And there was Kevin, too. She'd done the right thing there—she thought. But that again was something she couldn't really know. Not until it stopped hurting. . . .

The sound of the door being unlocked and opened brought her twisting round in bed, panic cramping her throat. Then she relaxed—of course, the cabin was two-berthed and presumably the other berth had been booked by someone else. Though she had checked with the purser on arrival, and he had told her that it was one of the few still vacant. That didn't mean it would stay that way, though, he had added with a harassed look at the queue mounting behind her, and Philippa had taken her key and slipped away, determined to settle herself in before any companion could join her.

This must be a latecomer, lucky enough to find a vacant berth. Philippa looked at the silhouette framed

5

in the doorway, hoping that the other woman, whoever she was, wouldn't be noisy or a smoker. That was the only trouble with booking a cabin, you never knew who you might have to share with. . . . And then her eyes widened in disbelief. That huge silhouette, blocking out most of the light from the passageway, couldn't be a *woman*! It was far too big, too broad. The wave of panic rose again as Philippa raised herself on one elbow, watching in horror as the bulky frame shifted, letting in more light for a brief moment before the cabin light was switched on and the door firmly closed.

There was an instant of silence while they both stared at each other. Philippa took in thick black hair with a white streak running back from one temple; piercing blue eyes under shaggy brows; a firm uncompromising mouth and a body that was built like a bear. She saw the sapphire eyes, equally startled, move quickly over her, assessing the dark hair that lay like a cap around her head, the brown eyes that could be as soft as a spaniel's, the slim hands that clutched the blankets to her small, pointed chin, and the slenderness of her body outlined under the bedclothes.

She found her voice at last and opened her mouth, meaning to point out this was her berth and he had obviously made a mistake. But before she could speak, the man's deep voice filled the tiny cabin, drowning any sound that Philippa could make.

'Just what in hell's name are you doing here?' he demanded, and the anger in his tone was unmistakable. 'And it's no use protesting that you're already in bed—that's a situation that can easily be remedied! And better had be, unless you want to spend the night with me.' His eyes moved over her again. 'Though on second thoughts, that could make the voyage more interesting,' he drawled.

Philippa felt the hot colour flood through her cheeks. Any chance of a civilised encounter was clearly out of the question. She wondered wildly if there were a steward within range—then set her teeth. Was there any reason why she couldn't deal with this—this *boor* herself? She was her own woman, wasn't she? She could cope with any male, and she'd proved that plenty of times.

'You seem to be under some misunderstanding,' she said coldly. '*I* booked this berth, five days ago. And there's no question of your sharing the cabin. You've obviously made a mistake and I'd be grateful if you'd leave at once. I'd like to get some sleep.' And she turned over, humping her back towards him, and waited for the light to go out.

It didn't. The next thing she knew was a heavy hand grasping her shoulder, forcing her back to look up in blazing indignation at the face that glowered down at her. Clearly, he was as angry as she, and Philippa quailed as she realised just how close he was—and how big. She wondered again if there was anyone within call—she felt peculiarly vulnerable, in bed with only a flimsy nightie and a blanket or two between her and this blatantly male stranger. But he surely wouldn't actually *do* anything to her—things like that didn't happen—or did they?

'Let go of me!' she gasped, wrenching uselessly at the hand that gripped her shoulder. 'I tell you, you've make a mistake—*I* booked this cabin!'

'And so did I,' he ground back at her. 'Cabin number sixty-four—right?' He watched her bewildered nod with satisfaction. 'So I recommend that you look again at your ticket. And then I'll turn my back like the perfect gentleman while you get up and get dressed and go to your *correct* cabin.'

'This *is* my correct cabin——'

'Then prove it.'

Philippa glared at him, then reached for her bag. But before her fingers touched the leather she jerked them back. Defiance firmed her chin as she raised her face to his.

'No. Why should I? I don't have to prove *anything* to you. And if you were the gentleman you say you are, you'd get right out of here and find the purser and tell him there's been a mistake, and get another berth—with a *man*!'

He handed her her bag, his eyes grim. 'Prove it, I

said. Or I may find I have to prove to you that I'm *not* a gentleman!'

Furiously, Philippa twisted open the bag and showed him her ticket. 'There you are. Cabin sixty-four. *Now* will you get out?'

He stared at it, black brows drawn together, then shrugged. 'No, I won't. Okay, so you're booked into cabin sixty-four—but, like I said, so am I. And I happen to know that there's not another vacant berth on the ship. I got the last.'

'Then that's just your hard luck, isn't it?' Philippa said sweetly. 'But I daresay you'll be able to find a seat.'

'I told you—I'm not getting out. Sorry about this, but I've as much right here as you have, and I intend staying until the ship docks at St Peter Port in the morning.'

He moved away and picked up the suitcase he had set down near the door, while Philippa stared at him, unable to believe her ears. He couldn't be calmly planning to stay here, in this cabin, *all night*—he just couldn't! He had to go—he had to be made to see reason.

'Look, you can't stay here,' she squeaked at last. 'There's been a mistake—you must see that. The purser wouldn't have put a strange man and woman together in a cabin—there's been some confusion. You'll have to go and see him—explain. They'll do something about it——'

'Like find me a seat, as you said.' He opened the case and took out a pair of navy pyjamas and a toilet-bag. 'But I don't intend to spend the night in a seat. I paid for a berth—there's a berth here—and that's good enough for me.'

'Well, it isn't for me!' Philippa blazed, sitting up with a jerk. The blankets fell away from her, revealing rosy breasts only just covered by the white lace of her nightie, and she blushed crimson as she caught the man's eyes on her, and lay down again hurriedly. Oh, what an awful position to be in! She felt so helpless—if only she could have stood up to him, literally, instead of being trapped here in this bed with nobody within call. She took a deep breath and started again. 'It isn't for me. I've never yet shared my bedroom with a man and I don't intend to start now. I booked and paid for this cabin two days ago—I wouldn't have minded sharing, if it was absolutely necessary, with a woman—but it's no part of my plan to share with you, so will you please put away your—your things and get out. Or I warn you, you'll be sorry!'

'Why, do you snore?' he enquired mildly. 'Or talk in your sleep? Never mind, I won't hold it against you. And I must admit I'm flattered at your confidences. So you're still an innocent virgin, are you? A rarity in this day and age, I believe. Well, you needn't worry, I wouldn't dream of disturbing your Sleeping Beauty innocence in that respect. But I'm afraid you're going to have to break your record and share the cabin with me. Because it isn't just *your* cabin, you see—it's *ours*. We've *both* booked and paid for it—and as I happen to know that there are no others and neither of us intends to spend a night in the lounge, then I suggest you stop these hysterics and resign yourself to the fact that we're here for the night. And I may add, I *don't* snore—or so several quite reliable sources inform me.' He shook out the dark blue pyjamas and Philippa watched, fascinated, as he began to strip off his shirt. 'And now,' he added, his head emerging, hair tousled, 'since you're such an innocent, might I further suggest that you turn your maidenly eyes away while I wash? I wouldn't like you to see anything that might frighten you——'

Before she could think, Philippa was out of the bed. Trembling with rage, she grabbed at his arms and tried to push him towards the door. There was no clear plan in her head—only a muddled conviction that if she could only take him by surprise she could get him out and lock the door against him. But, as she ought to have known, it was no use. He was like a rock—and as he stood, immovable, in the confined space of the cabin, Philippa realised with a shock of embarrassment that she was a lot closer to him than she wanted to be—and that a wave of sheer masculinity was emanating from him as she pulled at his arms, unaccountably weakening her muscles- and making her heart beat raggedly.

With a quick, lithe movement, he flicked his arms free of her grasp and then she found his hands holding her wrists. With a gasp of panic she twisted, trying to free herself, but his fingers were like steel, tightening as she struggled, and he drew her closer so that the warmth of his bare skin penetrated the thin cotton and lace that skimmed her body and his breath touched her cheek with a coolness that showed how hot she had become.

Philippa turned her head aside, disturbed by the feeling of that breath and the sensations it induced in her. Her heart was hammering now and she could feel the blood pounding in her ears. Her muscles were weak and her struggles feeble, and her breath quickened as she felt the iron hands draw her closer still, so that the dark hairs that covered his chest felt rough against her skin. She turned her head again, giving him a wild look from wide topaz eyes. The blue of his eyes pierced her and her lips parted with shock. Before they could close again, he had bent his head to hers and taken possession of them with his own.

A violent tremor ran through her and she would have fallen if he had not been holding her in that iron grasp. He released her wrists to slide his arms around her, keeping her firmly pressed against him, and she could feel the size and strength of his hard body against every inch of her own. Her mind reeled. Nobody—*nobody*— had ever kissed her like this before—demandingly, possessively, so that she felt plundered and invaded. Her arms hung limply at her side; her body felt boneless as she swayed in his arms, unable to prevent him from taking her lips. He played with them, his own mouth parting them, stroking them, manipulating and exploring. And then, when she thought she must faint, he finished with a tiny kiss on one corner and let her go.

Philippa staggered and fell back on the bed. Her heart was like a wild bird, beating frenziedly at the cage of her ribs. She looked up to see him watching her sardonically. There was no sign, in his cool mocking glance, of any equivalent of the bewildering tumult of sensation that still raged within her; no sign that her lips had been even the slightest bit disturbing to him; no hint that he too might have been aroused by unfamiliar, almost frightening sensations that he didn't know how to deal with.

But of course, he hadn't, had he. That kiss had been a mere demonstration as far as he was concerned; a demonstration of his superior strength and experience. A shiver of disgust passed over her.

'And now,' he said silkily, 'perhaps you'll stop this childish behaviour and get back into bed. There's nothing you can do about the situation. The ship's on her way now——' he glanced at his watch '—we'll be in Guernsey at six in the morning. All you have to do is turn over and go to sleep. So why don't you just do that?'

Philippa ran shaking fingers through her soft hair. Every instinct rebelled against this calm assumption that she would do what he wanted—from submitting to his kisses to allowing him to share her cabin. But what else could she do? He could win every time, through sheer strength, and though she might despise these tactics there was no way she could overcome them. All the same, she didn't have to pretend she liked it. With a toss of her head, she climbed back into bed and pulled the blankets around her again, looking up at him with bright defiance in her dark brown eyes.

'All right,' she said, keeping her voice icy. 'You win—this time. But if ever we meet again—and I hope to God we never do, but Guernsey's a small island and we might—don't expect to win a second time. I may not have your brawn, but I'm willing to take you on for brain any day—and you may find that sheer brute strength isn't quite enough when it comes to revenge.'

'My God, you really do enjoy a bit of drama, don't you!' he said, his voice tired. 'Revenge! What the hell does either of us want with revenge? There was never any need for argument in the first place—and if you'd been asleep when I came in we wouldn't have had it. So just pretend that's the way it was, will you? Close those pretty little pansy eyes and tell yourself it was all a dream.'

A nightmare, more like! But Philippa hastily closed her eyes as the stranger showed signs of divesting himself of the rest of his clothes, and a moment later she turned over. Perhaps if he thought she was asleep he wouldn't say or do anything else. And as the moments ticked by and the racing of her heart merged with the vibration of the engines, she told herself thankfully that she'd been right. There was no further word from her unwanted companion, nor did he touch her again. There were only the sounds he made as he washed; the creaking overhead as he climbed into the berth above her; the darkness when he finally switched off the light.

Philippa lay awake for a long time, acutely aware of the man who lay above her, his body less than a yard from her own. The quiet sound of his breath indicated that he had fallen asleep almost as soon as he had lain down. Clearly, he presented no risk after all, and she felt foolish at her panic. All the same, she told herself resentfully, anyone who was anything of a gentleman would have retreated immediately, leaving the cabin to her, whether it meant spending the night in a seat or not. She couldn't be blamed for objecting when he didn't.

She wondered how she would have reacted to him if they had met in any other circumstances. There was no doubt about it; he was a strikingly attractive man, the kind of man who would turn every female head wherever he went. The kind of man who would generally enjoy sharing his room with a woman—as he'd been quick to hint at. She shivered at the thought of what would have happened had she taken that hint.

It just showed that you couldn't be too careful. Imagine getting to know—and like—a man like him, without any idea of how he could really behave. Why, he was nothing but an animal! Probably he'd only restricted himself to a kiss tonight because he was tired—and knew that she would still be there in the morning.

Well, that was one thing he was wrong about,

Philippa told herself decisively. Because she *wouldn't* be there in the morning. And with any luck, small though Guernsey was, she would never see him again.

Determined though she was to stay awake, Philippa slept fitfully through the night, her dreams a jumble of unconnected pictures—pictures of her father and the house on Bethou, pictures of Kevin and that last evening when she had said goodbye to him—and pictures that brought her awake in panic, of a strange man bursting into her bedroom, huge against the light from outside, black-haired and blue-eyed with muscles like steel and lips that demanded total submission.

Throughout the night the engines hummed, a steady vibration that transmitted itself to her through the pillow. Luckily, the sea was calm. There had been a full moon just rising as they steamed quietly down Portsmouth Harbour, past the lights of the city and the moored ships, past the dimly-outlined masts of HMS *Victory* in her dry dock, past the glow of Gosport on the other side and out into the Solent. Buoys had flicked their warning lights and sounded their bells, and the Spithead Forts had loomed grim and shuttered at their side. The Isle of Wight had been a black mass, dotted with clusters of light, against the pale moonlit sky, and it was at that point that Philippa had come down to her cabin, relieved to find that there was apparently nobody sharing it, and ready to sleep until they reached Guernsey at dawn.

The man must have stayed on deck longer than she had, keeping his luggage with him rather than bringing it down to the cabin first as she had done. If only he had, the misunderstanding might have been cleared up without all that embarrassment caused by her being in bed when he arrived. Because obviously it *had* been a misunderstanding—quite an easy one too, considering the number of people who had been in that queue at the purser's office. There really wasn't much point in complaining about it.

All the same, he *could* have done the decent thing and gone back to the purser, even if it had meant having to sleep in a seat. And there'd been no need to kiss her like that—no need at all. . . .

Philippa shrugged herself impatiently around in the berth. Why did she have to keep *thinking* about him? He wasn't important, after all. She wasn't likely to meet him again. Presumably he was an ordinary holiday-maker, visiting Guernsey for a few days. He was nothing to do with her, or her life. And she had other things to think about that were.

Her father, for instance. She still hadn't come properly to terms with his death. Not that she was brokenhearted— he had been too remote for her to feel real grief now. But she could, and did, feel sadness over that remoteness. Should she have tried harder to break through the barriers he had erected between them— bring into his life the love and warmth he surely must have needed? Had she accepted too readily his ordering of her life, a life that kept her away from him too much, particularly as she grew older? Boarding-school, college, teaching—shouldn't she, at some point, have rebelled and come back to Guernsey for longer than the odd holiday and been a real daughter to the father who didn't seem to want one?

In her heart, Philippa knew that she *had* tried, over and over again, that there was no way to break through that barrier. But now that her father was dead and she would never be able to try again, she was suffering the remorse that came with knowing there would be no more chances. A remorse that was unfounded but nevertheless real. It was this that, apart from the funeral, had been her main reason for coming back to Guernsey; this, and the need to make decisions about the island and the house. And Kevin.

A movement overhead brought her back sharply to the present. For a few moments she had forgotten about the stranger. Moving quietly, she wriggled her arm out of the bed and peered at her watch. The luminous dial showed her that it was just after five, and she breathed a sigh of relief. By the time she had got up they would be serving breakfast in the restaurant. And in less than an hour she would be on Guernsey—her home, the island where she had been born.

A wave of unexpected excitement washed over her. It was two years since she had been home, two years since she had breathed the clear sea air of her island, seen the sun glinting off the boats in the harbour at St Peter Port. Her life in those years had been busy and full, and she hadn't thought she had really missed her home, where you were never far from the sea, where the stresses and strains of the mainland seemed remote and faintly ridiculous, where you couldn't go anywhere without meeting someone you knew.

Now, with landfall so near, she wasn't so sure. Otherwise, why should she be feeling so excited?

Twenty minutes later, dressed in slim-fitting jeans and a corduroy jacket, Philippa carried a tray of tea, cereal and toast over to a round table at the wide window that looked out over the bows of the ship. She had managed to dress and get herself and her suitcase out of the cabin without disturbing the stranger in the top berth. She hadn't been able to wash, of course—that would surely have woken him—and she felt grubby and only half awake, but at least she hadn't had to speak to him again, and hoped she never would. And the breakfast should make her feel better.

The full moon which had lit their way across the Channel now laid a path of glittering silver across the rippling sea. It hung like a guiding lantern in the sky, a globe of glowing pearl. Somewhere beneath it was Guernsey; and, conscious now of an increasing excitement, Philippa strained her eyes to catch her first glimpse of the island, wondering what changes she would see, what friends she would meet. Wondering too why she hadn't returned before—why she had thought that the mainland had more to offer. . . .

'So here you are! Beautiful morning, isn't it?'

Philippa jumped as if she had been stung. She knew those deep tones only too well—and they weren't those of a friend. She watched as her unwanted companion set his tray on her table, and spoke coldly.

'I tried not to disturb you.' In other words, I didn't want to have to speak to you again, she thought furiously. But the stranger seemed impervious to her hint. He smiled at her—and she had to admit his attraction, angry though she was—and settled himself comfortably in the chair beside her, swivelling it round so that he could follow her gaze out of the window. She couldn't help noticing his well-cut twill trousers, outlining the muscles of his thighs, and the pigskin jacket that spoke of money as clearly as the dull gold of the Cartier watch he wore on his wrist. Obviously rich—and probably thought himself far too good to travel with other passengers in the lounge.

'Be getting light in a few minutes,' he remarked conversationally. 'And we couldn't have had a better crossing, could we? By the way, I feel I should apologise for my rather—shall we say *brusque* temper last night? I'd had a pretty gruelling day—couldn't get a flight as I'd wanted to and only just managed to make the boat. It would have been the last straw to find myself without a bed.'

'That's quite all right,' Philippa said stiffly. So he'd been tired—did that excuse behaving like a barbarian? Forcing her to share the cabin with him against her will? But there was no point in reopening the issue. In less than half an hour they would be docking and she need never see him again.

'We don't even know each other's names, do we?' he continued, evidently without a scrap of embarrassment as he spread marmalade on his toast. 'I do think we ought to put that right. It doesn't seem at all the thing to spend a night together and part without even knowing what to call each other.'

Philippa glanced at him sharply. Was he mocking her? But his eyes were veiled by the thick black brows as he concentrated on his toast. She wanted to refuse to answer him, but there was little point in concealing her name after all. It couldn't *matter*.

'My name's Ozanne,' she said stiffly. 'Philippa Ozanne.'

To her surprise, he did look up then, his eyes meeting hers in a brief, startled glance. The blueness shook her again; she didn't remember ever having seen eyes of quite such a lancing blue. But she didn't see why he should look like that over mention of her name.

'It's quite a common name in Guernsey,' she said, a shade impatiently. 'There's nothing out of the ordinary about it.'

'No, I know,' he said thoughtfully. 'I've come across it before. You live on the island, then?'

'I was born there.' No reason why she should tell him her business—that her father had died, leaving everything to her, that she'd come back to sort it all out and decide what to do next. Certainly no reason why she should tell him that this had come just when she stood at one of life's crossroads anyway—and that it had proved an almost welcome bolthole from Kevin and the complications he had introduced into her life.

No, there was nothing she need tell this inquisitive stranger. But it might be as well to find out something about *him*—even if only to help her avoid any further meeting. Because that was something she could do without. The vibrations she had felt from him in the cabin a few hours earlier, the disturbing emanation of masculinity, were all things Philippa Ozanne could cope better without; life was complicated enough, without introducing yet another disturbing element.

'Well, I've told you my name,' she challenged him. 'What about returning the compliment?'

He seemed to come out of a reverie then, almost as if he had forgotten her presence, and she felt a twinge of pique. 'My name? Oh, I'm Zane Kendrick,' he said lightly. 'And look! Surely that's the island ahead? Just a few twinkling lights—but it's getting lighter every moment. Don't you feel excited—seeing your home after so long away?'

He rose to his feet and Philippa got up too, her breath quickening as the lights of St Peter Port drew steadily nearer. The sky was lightening now, a flush of pink spreading from the rising sun, behind them, to touch even the moon with an apricot glow that deepened every second. Philippa watched entranced as the darkness faded, leaving the sky an upturned bowl of warm peach, a suffusion of delicate colour that turned the sea to a sheet of hammered copper, rippling like a glowing carpet up to the dim shadow of the island.

The ferry ploughed steadily closer and the island grew clearer every second. Now Philippa could see the tiny houses that climbed the hill of St Peter Port above the harbour. She could see the masts of the boats that lay behind the harbour walls, sheltered from the storms that battered the island during the winter. Behind and beyond, the island humped its way inland to fields and hedges, the acres of glass that had once been built to grow grapes and now grew mostly tomatoes, but were still called vineries; the meadows where chestnut and white Guernsey cows still browsed and gave the islanders the rich, creamy milk that made them famous.

'Quite a sight, isn't it?' a deep voice murmured close to Philippa's shoulder. 'That little fairytale town with a Chinese lantern of a moon hanging over it in the dawn. Makes me go quite poetical!'

Philippa turned abruptly and picked her suitcase up with a jerk. Her mood was shattered and she felt nothing but an intense desire to get off this boat, away from this importunate stranger who didn't seem to know when he wasn't wanted. Once ashore, she would surely be able to escape him. And at least he couldn't follow her home. She didn't quite have a drawbridge to raise against him, but she had something just as good.

She didn't look round as she made her way to the position where the passengers were to disembark. Let him follow her if he liked—she wasn't going to give him the satisfaction of thinking she was interested. She wasn't, anyway—just intensely irritated. And, now that home was so near, unexpectedly excited at the thought of seeing it all again.

The ferry entered harbour slowly, creeping alongside the quay, and at last the passengers were free to leave. Philippa had calmed down a little by then; her pursuer had been blocked by two large women with several children and was several yards behind her in the queue. Philippa walked briskly down the steps and through the gateway, congratulating herself on her escape, then

groaned as she heard the purposeful steps close behind
her again.

'Thought it would be only polite to say goodbye
properly, especially after we've spent the night
together,' he announced far too loudly. 'By the way, are
you being met, or can I give you a lift? I've got a hire
car waiting.'

'Thank you, everything's organised,' Philippa said
coldly. 'I hope you have a good holiday, Mr—
Kendrick.' It was as near dismissal as she could make it.
But he didn't take the hint; merely grinned at her
infuriatingly and held out a large hand.

'Oh, I expect I will,' he said easily. 'Though I've some
business to attend to as well. Still, I don't expect to find
that anything but enjoyable. . . .' He took the hand that
Philippa reluctantly held out to him and she gasped as
she felt its strength and warmth, reminding her vividly
of the way he had held and kissed her last night.
Without pausing to wonder what his words meant, she
snatched her hand back again and transferred her
suitcase to it almost as a defence. For a moment she
stood there, irresolute. There was nothing now to
prevent her from giving him one last cool nod and
walking for ever out of his life. But she didn't. She
stayed there, half mesmerised by those cobalt eyes,
unable to make her brain give the order that would set
her legs in motion.

Then one of the large women, encumbered by a small
child and a large, untidy travelling-bag, lurched against
her and the spell was broken. Philippa gave the nod,
rather more wildly than she had intended, and turned
away almost in panic. Now that her legs were moving
they seemed to want to run, taking her at a fast stumble
out towards the quay where the taxis and hire cars
waited, and fishing-boats carried on their own business
oblivious to the landlocked world around them. St
Peter Port was light now, still flushed with pink as it
slowly awoke, still a magic town that held promise for
those it favoured. It smiled down on the harbour, the
boats and the fishermen. And, now that she had at last
rid herself of the man who had bedevilled her journey

and done his best to ruin her homecoming, Philippa felt that it smiled on her too.

With a little sigh of relief and relaxation, she set down her case. Her taxi was waiting, just as she'd arranged. And there, already out of it and striding along the quay to meet her, hand outstretched and a broad smile creasing his face, was Tommy Falla, whom she had known since she was a child. Tommy, who had been part of every leavetaking and homecoming since she had begun these journeys to and from the mainland. Tommy, her first and last link with home.

'Hullo, Tommy,' she exclaimed, shaking his hand. 'It's lovely to see you. Now I know I'm really on Guernsey again!'

'And not before time, either,' he reproved her. 'Susan was saying only a while ago that it was a long time since you'd been home. We'd no idea then, of course——'

'No, of course not,' Philippa broke in quickly. 'I understand it was all very sudden. I would have come at once if I'd known he was so ill, but you know what he was like.'

Tommy nodded as he stowed her luggage into the boot of the taxi. 'Even Hubert never really realised,' he said. 'But it's always the same when you see someone every day, you don't notice the changes. Now, are you going straight out to the house?'

'Yes, please.' Philippa climbed in beside him and shut the door. 'The tide's all right, is it?'

'Yes, you've got until ten.' Tommy settled himself in his seat, taking up rather more room than he had on Philippa's last visit. Susan's good cooking showing results at last, Philippa thought in some amusement. She wondered whether the Guernseywoman's sister-in-law, Margaret, had persuaded her father to eat more as well, in his last year or two. Or had he still been obstinately leaving half of every meal that had been taken across to him? He was lucky to have had anyone willing to do so much—his refusal to have anyone doing more than the essential cleaning in the house would have led to his starvation if Margaret hadn't been as obstinate as he.

She sat back and feasted her eyes on her surroundings as Tommy manoeuvred the car along the quay towards the town. Early though it was, the harbourside was bustling with people, most of them off the ferry. Some were hailing taxis, some settling themselves cautiously into unfamiliar hire cars, some setting out to walk to their destination. Philippa let her eyes stray over them, amused by the variety of people who chose to visit Guernsey. The thinking man's Jersey, someone had called it. Her lips twitched; then she stiffened.

Just at the side of the quay, hefting his case into a smart-looking Renault with the yellow H badge on the bumper that denoted it was a hired car, was the man who had shared her cabin last night. As Tommy's taxi crept past, he glanced up and saw Philippa sitting inside it. Their eyes met. Philippa felt again that disturbing wave of sensation that had threatened to overwhelm her when she had shaken his hand a few moments earlier. Then he grinned that infuriating and dazzling grin and Philippa turned her head away sharply.

Don't let him affect you that way, she admonished herself. He's nothing to you—with luck you'll never see him again. Forget him. There's enough to think about.

And as Tommy turned left on the main road and headed up the long hill leading out of St Peter Port, she deliberately shut Zane Kendrick out of her mind and began to think instead of the other problems that confronted her. Like what she was going to do about her home—and whether she was ever going to be able to forget Kevin.

The journey across the island was short and every yard of it was familiar to Philippa, bringing memories crowding back. So many times she had made this journey, sitting beside Tommy. He had been the one to take her to the airport for her first flight to the mainland. She had been only thirteen then, frightened and rebellious, unable to understand why her father should have suddenly decided to send her to school on the mainland. Until then he had seemed perfectly satisfied with her progress at the island school. It was only when she had put on that new dress that she had had made for the school dance that he had looked at her with eyes that seemed to see ghosts and sent her out of the room. After that, nothing had been the same, and then he had told her one day that she was to go to school in England.

'But why?' she had protested. 'I don't see why. I like it here. My friends are here. I don't *want* to go away!'

'It will be better for you,' he said, almost as if he hadn't heard her. 'The Abbey School is a very good one and you'll soon make new friends. It will be good for you to see that there are other places besides Guernsey. Children become too narrow-minded if they stay here all their lives.'

'*You've* stayed here all your life,' she said instantly, and as instantly saw that he was proof of his own words. 'I don't even know where it is—Malvern. It's in the middle of nowhere!'

'It's very near the middle of England,' he corrected her. 'Don't argue, Philippa. It's all arranged. You're to start next term.'

Philippa had, of course, continued to argue and to plead, but nothing had changed her father's inflexible attitude. And since then, three times a year, she had made this journey across the island, travelling usually by air to Birmingham and by car to the spa town of Malvern, set on the side of a long, rolling hill on the border of Worcestershire and Herefordshire. From her bedroom window in the school she had had a view across the chessboard plain of Worcestershire, with Bredon Hill like a stranded whale in the middle distance and the blue shadow of the Cotswolds beyond. Such a view would have been impossible on Guernsey; most of that distance would have been sea. But here, the sea was two hundred miles away.

Gradually she had become resigned and accustomed to her new life. The countryside surrounding the school was pleasant enough, though she never grew to know it intimately—the school rules were too strict for more than the occasional walk or picnic on the hills. From the other side of the long ridge you could look towards the Welsh mountains, but Philippa had never, during her schooldays, penetrated so far.

Later, she had left school and gone to a teachers' training college, and from there to her first job in a small country primary. The thought of returning to Guernsey, once so urgent, had crossed her mind from time to time, but she had told herself that she needed more experience, that it mightn't be possible to get a teaching job on the island anyway. A couple of years had drifted by in this way, with Guernsey like a shadow on the horizon, a place to be returned to some day but not just yet, not for a while.... And then she had moved to Coventry, to the back-street school full of tough children in a multi-racial area, where everyone's problems were worse than her own and you either got absorbed or got out.

Philippa had become absorbed. And then she had met Kevin.

She had first met Kevin Brant when he came to collect his daughter, Vicci, from school. Philippa had been helping the child with her duffle coat when he came into the classroom, and she had looked up in surprise at the tall man with his sleek fair hair and half-shy, boyish smile.

'Daddy!' The child twisted away from her and ran over to him. 'This is my daddy,' she had explained proudly. 'Mummy's gone away, so he's looking after me now. Daddy, this is my teacher, Miss Ozanne. It's a funny name, isn't it, but she comes from an island. Fancy living on an *island*!' There was awe in the childish voice, and Kevin Brant grinned.

'Could have a lot to recommend it,' he said, and Philippa noticed that his voice was light and pleasant. She got to her feet, feeling suddenly awkward. That reference to the child's mother having 'gone away'— what did it mean? A simple visit to relatives or friends—or something more sinister? She'd noticed little Vicci looking rather subdued just lately.

However, it wasn't a question she could ask, and she

smiled and held out her hand. 'Your daughter's a credit to the class, Mr Brant,' she told him. 'The first to write her name! Go and get your work-book to show your daddy, Vicci.'

The child ran to her desk in a corner of the room and Philippa glanced up to find Kevin Brant looking down at her with an odd expression in his eyes. It made her feel breathless and she felt the colour warm her cheeks. She was glad to turn to the child and help her turn the pages of the book.

After that, Vicci's father came in to collect her every afternoon, usually a few minutes later than the other parents, and it became accepted that he should fetch Vicci from the classroom. He and Philippa had a few moments' more conversation each time and she began to like him. More than that, she began to realise that he liked her.

'Look, Miss Ozanne,' he said at the end of that first week, 'I'd like to have a talk with you. I need some advice, about Vicci. I suppose there's no chance that you're free tonight?'

'Well. . . .' Philippa hesitated. 'I'm not actually doing anything, but——'

'Then would you spare me some time?' He looked awkward. 'I'd like to ask you to come round to my home, but it's a little difficult just now. . . . Could we meet somewhere, have a meal perhaps?' He caught her expression. 'I ought to tell you that Vicci's mother—well, I don't think she's coming back. I really would like to talk to you, Miss Ozanne. You know Vicci better than anyone else.'

Philippa had given in—and that was how it had all begun. She was sure even now that Kevin had never intended to start an affair with her. That first request for help—that had been genuine enough. And they had discussed Vicci that first evening as they ate Chinese food. But they'd talked about other things too; they'd laughed at each other's attempts to use chopsticks, compared likes and dislikes, discovered all kinds of things they had in common. They had enjoyed that first evening—enjoyed it too much not to repeat it.

After all, Philippa had told herself, it was for Vicci's sake that she went on seeing him—keeping a close contact. The child must be missing her mother. It behoved them all to do their utmost to make her life as happy and full as possible.

But it hadn't been very long before she had to admit that she was deeply in love with Kevin Brant. And that discovery had scared her. She had always prided herself on her high principles. *She* was never going to have affairs with married men. She wasn't even going to have affairs, come to that. She was the old-fashioned kind— she'd keep herself for the man she married.

To discover now that she was in love with another woman's husband, father of one of her own pupils, shook her badly. It was even worse when Vicci, staying in one playtime because of a cold, confided that she had seen her mother again.

'She might be coming back soon,' the child told her, her small face alight with hope. 'I hope it won't be long. Daddy doesn't really know how to cook, you know.'

Philippa stared at the trusting eyes and went cold. Kevin had never mentioned the possibility of his wife's returning. He'd told Philippa that he no longer loved Vivien, that he would soon be filing for divorce. Philippa's own uneasiness had been dispelled by his assurances that the marriage had been broken up long before she came on the scene, that no one could ever accuse her of being the 'other woman'. He'd made a mistake, he said, that boyish look on his face making Philippa want to draw him to her and comfort him. Was he to be punished for that mistake for the rest of his life?

Now, it seemed that everything had changed. Vivien wanted to come back—and Philippa was standing in her way. As long as she remained on the scene, the marriage could not be repaired. She would become a home-breaker—the other woman. And at that, she balked.

Philippa spent that night awake and by morning she knew that she had to give up Kevin. He *had* loved his wife, once. That love could be resurrected. And there was Vicci—she needed her mother, and Philippa could not bring herself to be the one to deprive Vicci of either of her parents.

Last of all, there were Philippa's own principles. So far, she had managed to hold back from making that final commitment to Kevin. She could give him up now and salvage her self-respect, if nothing else. Go ahead and other people would get hurt.

It was the hardest thing Philippa had ever done when she told Kevin she didn't want to see him again. The pain wasn't assuaged in the least by knowing she had done the right thing. It hurt her every day when she saw Vicci in class, knowing by the child's increasing lightheartedness and stability that her mother must be back. It hurt when she went home alone to a long empty evening. It hurt when she woke to a new day, knowing that it would be as painful as all the others.

The news that her father had died and she would have to return to Guernsey, at least temporarily, came almost as a relief. There, at least, she might be able to forget the pain of the past few weeks.

'Nearly there now.' Tommy had always been blessedly silent on these journeys, seeming to understand that she needed quiet either to reintroduce herself to the island or to say goodbye. He waved a hand at the hedges. 'See many changes?'

'Not a lot.' Philippa's lips parted in eagerness as her heart suddenly jerked with excitement as they rounded the last corner. In a moment they would be in sight of the sea again—running down the coast road, looking out at Vazon Bay—turning to go out to the point—and then the island would be in view at last, small and rocky and green.

Her father's fortress. The home to which he had retreated when everything went wrong. The home in which he had brought up his daughter—and from which he had sent her when she started to become a woman.

'Bethou,' Philippa murmured, her voice soft with memories, and Tommy glanced at her sharply.

'Ah, Bethou,' he agreed noncommittally. 'There she is. And if you'd like to walk over by yourself, I'll put your luggage in the tractor and Hubert will see to it when he's had his breakfast. I daresay you'll not be wanting any.'

'I had some on the ferry,' Philippa said absently, though that seemed a long time ago now. Her eyes were fixed on the tiny island with its granite house growing from the rocks above the shoreline. It lay just far enough off the coast to qualify for its name, and at high tide was a true island, separated from the main island of Guernsey by a strip of rock-infested water. But now, like its sister island of Lihou farther down the coast, it was accessible on foot by way of a paved and rocky causeway that led between the clutter of boulders of the seabed.

Philippa got out of the taxi and gazed across the strait. The sun was fully up and shed its clear, early-morning light full on the island. There was nobody else about. The sand gleamed with the retreating tide and clumps of dark brown seaweed masked the rocks. On the island, nothing stirred, but she knew there would be rabbits in the grass and birds picking daintily along the shoreline.

She forgot all about Tommy. She walked as if in a daze, down the beach, on to the paved causeway, following its track down the sand and between the glittering pools. Her body was shaken by emotion; she was returning home in very different circumstances from those of earlier days. This time, it could be for good. This time, there would be no silent father there to break her heart.

Bethou had always been her home. But now there was a difference. It was *hers*—hers to do with as she wished.

And nobody—*nobody*—could argue with whatever decision she chose to make.

# CHAPTER TWO

By the time she reached the island Philippa's shoes were wet, but she scarcely registered the fact. Her eyes were fastened on the grey house, built of Guernsey granite, the house that her grandfather had built over sixty years ago after his second marriage. It stood firm and solid, its feet securely rooted in the island from which it seemed to have grown rather than been built. Here she had been born and spent her childhood; back to this house she had come for her holidays after she had been sent to the school on the mainland. Here, her father too had been born, had grown up and brought his bride; had lived, as husband and widower, in an increasingly bitter loneliness until he died.

Slowly Philippa walked up the beach, across the rocks, to the grass that sloped down in front of the walls. The house itself was like a small fortress, built on an enclosed knoll, its high walls surrounding the garden that gave its inhabitants even more privacy—a privacy that was necessary, when anyone could cross at low tide from the mainland. Occasionally, too, stragglers would be stranded when the tide rose more swiftly than they had expected, even though as on Lihou the times were marked daily on a blackboard close to the causeway. There were always a few who had forgotten that time and tide wait for no man and were slightly indignant to discover that ten minutes on a swiftly rising tide made all the difference.

Hubert had left the garden door unlocked, and Philippa opened it and went inside. She looked sadly at the lawn where she had played as a child. It was neglected and overgrown, the grass lank and stringy like unwashed hair. The borders that Hubert had worked on with such care were full of weeds already and the whole place had a desolate, unloved air about it.

Of course, Hubert and Margaret were both getting old.

Philippa would have expected younger help to have been employed, but it didn't look as if this were so. She felt a stab of guilt that she didn't know more, that she hadn't been back to see for herself how her father was and what was happening to her home. But then she hadn't been exactly encouraged, had she? On her last visit her father had been more remote than ever, so that she had spent the time alternately trying to break through the barrier he had erected around himself, and vowing never to come here again until he asked her. It was too hurtful, seeing this father she longed to love shut himself so deliberately away from her. There was a limit to how much pain of that kind one could expose oneself to.

And as time went on there had been more and more to occupy her on the mainland. Her studies, her friends, her job—and Kevin. For the past month he had taken up her thoughts almost to the exclusion of anything else; and Guernsey and its tiny island, with the lonely man living out his strange embittered life, had seemed very far away.

The front door, large and heavy, hadn't altered since she had last seen it, except to become shabbier. With misgiving in her heart, Philippa turned the iron handle and opened it, then stepped into the hall.

Margaret had obviously been here. Her welcome glowed in the bowl of primroses that stood on the little hall table that had been Philippa's mother's. There was a smell of polish too, and the window that let in light beside the door was clean and sparkling.

But none of this could take away the faint mustiness that lay over everything, the staleness of the air that came down the stairs, the chill of a house that had not known love or laughter for years; only an increasing sadness and disillusion.

It took Philippa some time to explore the whole house, and by the time she had finished she felt the heavy weight of depression bearing down upon her own spirits. It was as if that unhappy ghost still haunted the house, filling the rooms with a gloom and weariness that nothing would dispel. And there were her own memories to add to the general despondency.

Many of the rooms had clearly not been used for years. Probably no one had been into the sitting-room since her own last visit, and the dining-room looked equally abandoned. Margaret's efforts at welcome hadn't extended here, Philippa noted. She would hardly have had time in the few days since Colin Ozanne's death. Sheets still covered the furniture and when Philippa drew back the curtains the dust made her choke. The big stone fireplace was empty except for the debris that had dropped into it from the cold chimney above, and Philippa remembered the driftwood she had collected to burn here, the bright blue salty flames she had gazed into.

Her father seemed to have lived mainly in the kitchen. That, at least, had an air of having been used, though many of the pots and pans had gathered a dull film that indicated little cooking had been done here. He would have lived on bread and cheese for years if he had been allowed, Philippa reflected. It was as if he had lost interest in life a long time ago and wanted no more than to go through the motions until he could leave it.

Upstairs, the air of neglect was just the same. Unfurnished rooms where dust lay on the floorboards; and only two rooms that could be used at all—her father's, bleak and cold with its one narrow bed and minimum of furniture, and her own, with the wide bed that had been moved in there only days after her mother's death and her own birth. That had been the beginning of Colin Ozanne's bitterness, when he had lost his wife with the same stroke of fate that brought him a daughter instead of a son. Philippa looked at the two rooms. Here was something that could be changed at once. Not her own room—that, alone of all the rooms in the house, had been stamped with her own personality. But her father's room—all that cold, unhappy furniture could go and she would replace it with something warm and welcoming, something that said yes to life instead of no. As the whole house, changing under her possession, would do. . . .

As she went downstairs again, it struck her with some force that she was thinking as if she meant to stay here.

But she had never made any decision about that—it was something she had left, something she had told herself she couldn't decide until she saw the place again. And nothing that she had seen so far had been in the least encouraging. In fact, if she had any sense at all, she thought as she opened the kitchen door, she would go straight back at once, see her father's advocate in St Peter Port and put the house and the island up for sale. It was really the only thing to do—wasn't it?

Margaret had added a few stores to the cupboards and Philippa found a jar of instant coffee and some milk. She put the kettle on, thankful that her grandfather had installed electricity, and spooned coffee into a large pottery mug. There was a packet of biscuits, too, and she ate one while she waited for the kettle to boil. It seemed a very long time since breakfast.

The kitchen was chilly, with no sun shining through its windows, and Philippa took her coffee and biscuits out into the garden. Parts of it were still pretty, with spring flowers rampant in the long grass. A patch of primroses lay like a pool of fallen sunlight, violets glowed like a scrap of rich velvet. Daffodils and narcissi bobbed their fragile heads in the morning breeze and there were already tiny buds on the climbing roses and the fuchsias that smothered the wall.

Philippa perched herself on the edge of the old well. Water had been brought out to the island years ago, but Hubert had always used well-water for the garden. She looked around her, wondering just why the place looked so neglected. Had Hubert been ill, unable to work, or had he left her father to work for someone else? No, it couldn't be that—Tommy would have said so. Tommy was Hubert's brother and knew all his business. But something was obviously wrong. Unless it was merely that her father had become such a recluse in the last year or so that he had simply refused to have any work done about the place at all.

Finishing her coffee, Philippa went back into the house. Whether or not she was going to stay here, there were things that had to be done. She needed to find out what the arrangements were for her father's funeral tomorrow. She would have to look again through that store cupboard and decide what provisions she required, at least for the next few days. And she wanted to have another look at those bedrooms.

Her own room was much as she had left it. Margaret had made up the big bed and the carpet had been brushed and the furniture dusted. Philippa crossed to look out of the window at the familiar view of Guernsey, separated from Bethou by a clutter of wet rocks and seaweed. Later, that rocky strip would be filled by the racing tide and nobody would be able to reach her, except by boat. She could understand her father's retreat into solitude. It was all too easy for such a thing to happen, when your home was cut off from all others for twelve hours a day.

His room had faced out to sea, away from Guernsey, and Philippa opened his door and stood looking round. Towards evening the room would be filled with the golden light of sunset, but now it was dim and chilly and there was nothing but sea outside the window. Her grandfather had built the house on the highest point of the tiny island; looking down she could see the wilderness of a garden and, beyond the wall, the grassy tumps which had been nibbled short by the few sheep that were kept there, and the rabbits. The shoreline was marked all around by rocks; a huge pile to the west, almost like a ruined castle, a cliff about thirty feet high on the northern point, a more sheltered bay towards the east. But if you sat in the hard chair, as her father had so often done, and stared straight out of the window, it was only sea that you looked upon.

Philippa shivered. She would have to get this room cleared. It's sombre atmosphere was pervading the whole house. It wouldn't take long. There was little furniture—a small chest of drawers, the bedside table, the chair and the bed itself. She went back to her own room and looked out of the window. Yes, there was Hubert, coming across the causeway with her luggage in the trailer behind the tractor, just as Tommy had promised. He could take some of the furniture back with him. She could make a start on that, at least.

Perhaps then she would feel better and the house feel less oppressive.

Working quickly, she pulled the drawers out from the chest and took them into her own room to tip the contents on the bed. They were pathetically little—a few clothes, personal belongings, and some small, leather-bound books that she had never seen before. One of them fell open as she tipped it on to the bed and she saw that the yellowed pages were filled with smooth, copperplate handwriting.

Curiously, Philippa picked it up. A diary! She flipped through the pages, wondering who had kept it and what they had written about. Maybe it would be a good idea to find out. It might be written by her grandfather or grandmother. It might even help her to understand her own father, that strange, difficult man who had given her life and now had bequeathed her an island. It would be interesting to read a record of their daily life in this isolated place.

By the time Hubert had brought his tractor and trailer across to the shore, Philippa was waiting for him, the smaller pieces of her father's furniture already in the hall. She ran down the beach to meet the old man, a little anxious as to what changes might have taken place, but to her relief he too was just the same, oddly like his brother Tommy, a short peardrop of a man with a thousand wrinkles and a jowly chin. He climbed down from the tractor and shook her hand warmly.

'It's been a long time, Miss Philippa,' he declared. 'Too long. I don't say as you should have come before, not with things as they were, but some of us have missed you.'

'I've missed you too, Hubert,' said Philippa, realising with some surprise that this was the truth. 'And Margaret. And I've missed Bethou, too.' She turned and looked at the grey house behind her, seeing it with different eyes. The strangeness was wearing off and familiarity taking its place. She had only been on the island for an hour or so, yet already she was beginning to feel that she had never been anywhere else.

'Once an islander, always an islander,' Hubert said

robustly. 'You can't tell me there's anything on the mainland that's better than here on Guernsey. People say they wouldn't like to live here, they'd feel trapped. What I say is, what do you want with hundreds of miles of land all around you? It only means more and more people. I like the sea round me. You know where you are with the sea.'

Philippa smiled. 'You could have something there,' she agreed, thinking of the teeming crowds of Coventry. 'And how's Margaret? She made the house lovely and welcoming, with the flowers, and the groceries, and my room looks as if I'd never left it.'

'Ah, well, she wanted you to feel at home,' Hubert said gruffly, and in that sentence revealed his and Margaret's knowledge that Bethou had never been a real home to Philippa. Their little cottage on the main island had been that more than this granite house. 'She'll be over later on to get you a meal,' he added, turning to the trailer. 'I'll just get these bits and pieces in now.'

'Yes, and there are some things I'd like you to take back, please.' Philippa lifted down her travelling bag while Hubert took the suitcase. 'The furniture from my father's room. I'd like you to have it, if it's any use to you.'

Hubert stared at her. 'Your father's furniture? But you can't go giving that away, Miss Philippa. Not until the will and everything's sorted out. And anyway—it don't seem right, not so soon——'

'I really don't want it in the house,' Philippa told him firmly. 'Or even on the island. Please, Hubert. It probably doesn't mean a thing to you, but to me—well, it makes me shiver. Please take it away. If it makes you feel happier, you can consider it still mine until everything's settled, but I promise you it will be all right. *Would* it be any use to you?'

Hubert considered. 'Well, our back bedroom is a bit bare,' he admitted. 'Margaret gave the furniture to our Hetty when she got married and somehow we've never replaced it. We just have one of those camp beds in there. But your father's things—well, I don't know. . . .'

'Well, just look after it for me, would you? I really would feel happier with it gone. Look, I've brought some of it down already, there's only the main part of the chest and the bed to bring and they're both quite light, just a bit awkward. Let's take it all out straightaway, shall we, and then I'll make some coffee and you can tell me all that's been happening while I've been away. . . .'

Still clearly uneasy but swept away by Philippa's determination, the old man helped her carry the last two pieces of furniture down the stairs and out to the beach. To Philippa's relief, they were able to fit everything on the trailer; then, glancing at her watch, she declared that there was just time for coffee before the tide began to come in again and covered the causeway.

As they drank their coffee, Hubert told Philippa the details of her father's funeral next day. The family advocate, Henry Batiste, had made the arrangements and Philippa knew that he would want to see her afterwards. By then she would have a better idea of her own plans, she thought, and looked out again at the neglected garden.

'What happened to my father in the last two years, Hubert?' she asked softly. 'I know he never liked to have too much fuss around him, but he always took care of the house and garden. Now, it looks—well, as if he'd lost all interest.'

Hubert shrugged. 'I suppose that's just what he did, Miss Philippa. Anyway, he let me and Margaret do less and less about the place. Upset us both to see it all going down the way it has, but what can you do when a man refuses to let you do what's needed? He cut our hours down, you see, and we just had to get work with other people. We didn't want to—our family's always been tied up with the Ozannes—but what else could we do? We had to live.'

His old face looked so distressed that Philippa longed to comfort him. Impulsively, she reached across the table and laid her hand over his, feeling the roughness that spoke of years of hard work. 'Of course you had to,' she told him. 'And I'm sure it wasn't for any reason against you that Dad did that. It was just—well, his state of mind, I suppose.' She couldn't be more specific than that, but she knew that Hubert would understand.

He nodded. 'Ah, that'd be right, Miss Philippa. His state of mind wasn't so good, these last years. He'd got very bitter, you see. I don't think he even knew what he was so bitter about in the end. All those old quarrels— it does no good to harbour a grudge like that. It did him the most harm in the end, after all.'

'I never really understood about all that,' said Philippa. 'I wish you'd tell me what it was all about, Hubert.'

The old man avoided her soft eyes. 'Well, I don't know so much about it myself really,' he said evasively. 'Happened before my time, as you might say. And it don't do no good to go repeating those old stories. All I know is it was over land and money, and there's more bitterness over those two things than anything else.'

'Is there? More even than love?'

'Ah, love! There's a lot of nonsense talked about love. But whatever bitterness that causes, people can get over it. Quarrels over land go on for generations, and that's what happened on Bethou. That started with your grandfather, old Philippe Ozanne, that you were named after, and he handed it down to your father, and that's what caused the strife between him and his brother. Better forgotten now, all that is.'

'But I've a right to know,' Philippa exclaimed. 'My father hardly ever spoke of all this to me—and now I own Bethou surely I ought to know its history. You're the only one who can tell me, Hubert.'

Her brown eyes pleaded with him and the old man gave in. He sighed heavily.

'I can't tell you much, even so,' he warned her. 'All I know is that there was a quarrel between old Philippe and his first son, Raoul. Raoul left him—went to the mainland—and never came back. So Philippe left his property to his second son, Colin, which he was entitled to do, having married Colin's mother—that was Susan, your grandmother—after Raoul left the island. His first wife, Adele I think *her* name was, died when Raoul was still a baby.'

He told the story baldly, as if he wanted to get it over with as soon as possible, but Philippa's sensitive imagination caught at once the sadness behind his words. She sat silent, thinking of the bitterness that there must have been between father and son—why? What had gone wrong between them?—and the loneliness of the man who had lost first his wife and then his son. But he'd married again, and had another son. Life hadn't been a total loss. And he'd built the house on Bethou to be a family home.

'But why should *my* father be bitter about that?' she asked, frowning, 'nobody had done him any harm.'

'Well, I don't think it was that really. He was all right until your mother died. Maybe he just caught the habit from your grandfather—he never forgot the way his first boy had gone off and left him and the house was never a happy one. And when things went wrong for your father too—your mother dying like that, so early, and you not being a boy, not that that was your fault or hers, come to that—well, I suppose it was easy for him to slip into the same ways.'

'A sort of inherited tendency?' Philippa shivered. 'I hope I haven't inherited it too!'

The faded blue eyes softened as they looked at her. 'Not you,' Hubert said. 'You take after your mother, you do—always have. It was a pleasure to have your bright little face around the place, and at one time I thought your father felt that way too. Until you started to grow up and looked more like her than he could be comfortable with.'

'And that's why he sent me away to school.' Philippa spoke slowly. Things were becoming clearer to her now and her heart ached for the lonely man who had been her father. Her eyes misted with tears.

Hubert got up. 'I'll have to be going now, Miss Philippa, or I won't get the tractor across.' He hesitated, as if unwilling to leave. 'Now, are you sure you'll be all right here? You can come with me if you like and have your dinner. Margaret will be pleased to see you.'

'I want to see her, too,' said Philippa. 'But I'll come over later, if you don't mind. I'd like to get my things sorted out and settle in here—get to know the place again. The boat's down on the beach, isn't it?'

'It is. Well, you came over whenever you feel ready, Miss Philippa.' They walked out into the garden together. 'And I'll try to put in a few hours at this at the weekend, if you'd like me to. I don't like seeing it run wild any more than you do.'

'That's good of you, Hubert.' Philippa shook his hand again, glad to be back with the man she had known ever since she was born. 'And I'll see you tomorrow, anyway. After that, we should be able to see our way a bit clearer.'

Hubert climbed up into his tractor and chugged away across the causeway. Already the tide had turned and water was seeping across the winding track. In a few minutes it would be impassable. Philippa would be quite alone on her island.

She turned to go back to the house, then stopped still, her hand flying to her mouth in dismay. For she wasn't alone at all—nor would be for several hours, unless she did something very quickly indeed. And after her previous experience, only hours ago, she didn't have a lot of confidence in her ability to succeed this time.

Zane Kendrick was standing at the head of the beach, watching her, his dark face inscrutable, his searing blue eyes hooded under shaggy brows. Black hair swept back from his high forehead, winged at one side with silver. He stood tall and loose-limbed, totally at ease, able to handle any situation.

Able, Philippa thought sickly, to handle her. . . .

She took a deep breath, smoothed suddenly damp palms down the sides of her jeans, and raised her chin. This was *her* island, she reminded herself—her own private property. Here, on these few acres of land, she ruled supreme—Queen of the Castle.

'Good morning,' she said coldly, as if she'd never met the man before, never spent a night sharing the same cabin with him. 'You know, of course, that Bethou is private property? I like everyone to be off during high tide. And as you can see that the tide is coming in quite quickly now, perhaps you'd be good enough to go. Or you may be stranded here for several hours.'

The firm lips twitched and a glint of mockery showed in the cobalt eyes, but the stranger made no movement. If anything, he seemed somehow to settle himself even more firmly on the rock where he stood, and Philippa felt her irritation turn to anger.

'Please,' she said, battling to keep her voice cool. 'I've asked you to go. You'll get very wet if you don't leave at once. The tide comes in very quickly.'

'I believe you,' he said, his voice deep and smooth— and was that a hint of *amusement* in it? Damn him, what was there to laugh at? 'But as it happens I don't want to go just yet.'

'You don't *want*——' Again, Philippa fought to keep control of herself. What was it about this man that got under her defences like this? She was normally even-tempered enough, wasn't she? Well—most of the time, anyway. She bit her lip and started again.

'I'm afraid it isn't what you want that matters,' she told him flatly. 'This is my property and I'm asking you to leave it. At once—while you still can. Or you will be marooned here for several hours, and I'm sure you don't want that any more than I do.'

'How can you be so sure?' He *was* laughing at her! 'It was always one of my dreams to be stranded on a desert island with a beautiful girl. Now it's happening—how many people have their wildest dreams come true, do you suppose? Has it ever happened to you, for instance?'

'Oh, you—you——' Baffled and furious, Philippa gave up. She turned her head to look behind at the strand between Bethou and the main island. Water was covering it more rapidly every minute and she knew that even now it could be dangerous to attempt the crossing. But that was *his* lookout!

'Look, you've got about five minutes,' she snapped. 'Go now and you'll just about make it. Otherwise——'

'Otherwise?' His voice was soft and his eyes raked her slim figure in the blue jeans and T-shirt that hugged every slender curve. Philippa felt suddenly scared. All right, he hadn't touched her last night—except for that searing kiss, the memory of which still brought a deep crimson colour flooding up from her throat. But there had been people around on the ship—other passengers, the stewards. Here on Bethou there was no one—nor would there be anyone for several hours. And he must have seen Hubert leave in his tractor. He would *know* that she was alone.

'Otherwise I'll call someone to remove you,' she said, her voice suddenly husky. 'We do have a telephone. And now, if you'll let me pass——'

Her heart thudded as she tried to slip past him, but almost as she had known he would, he shot an arm out and caught her easily. His long fingers wrapped themselves round her narrow wrist, jerking her towards him so suddenly that she fell against him and was for a moment acutely conscious of the hard, muscular body. Then she wrenched herself upright, holding herself stiffly away and glared furiously into the steel-blue eyes.

'Let go at once!' Somewhere at the back of her mind was relief that her dismay didn't show in her voice as she went on scathingly: 'You may think that just because there's no one else around you've got me at your mercy, but oh, you're so wrong. Brute force won't get you anywhere with me, Mr Kendrick. Now, will you please get off my island and stop *harassing* me? What is it with you, anyway? Don't you know any other way to spend a holiday than to follow girls around?'

At this he flung back his head and roared with laughter, while Philippa bit her lip and stared angrily at the ground. How was it that she always seemed to make a fool of herself with this man? No matter what she said or did it always came out wrong, and he was the winner all along the line. She pulled at her arm and tried to break his grip with the fingers of her free hand, but it was no use. He didn't even seem to notice.

'Okay, stop panicking,' he said at last, calming down. 'I'm not going to rape you. Or even make passionate love to you—not today, at any rate.' He looked at her and his mouth twitched again. 'You know, you should try not to be so much on your dignity. It makes me just long to put you down a little. Now——' he released her arm '—you're not going to run away, are you? After all, there's nowhere to run to. And our little argument seems to have settled itself, since I think even you will agree now that I've left it too late to cross back over the causeway. So why don't we bury the hatchet and make friends? You could even offer me coffee.'

'Why ever didn't *I* think of that?' Philippa said sarcastically as she turned to look back again across the strait. She had to admit that he was right—even she couldn't insist on his crossing that wide, ever-deepening stretch of water with its swirling currents. So she was to be blessed with his company for the rest of the day, was she? Well, she didn't *have* to invite him into the house. It was his fault he'd got stranded here—he could figure out his own way of passing the time.

'Well,' she said, turning back to the stranger with a sudden dazzling smile, 'you seem to have got your wish. Stranded on a desert island. Have a nice day!' And with a quick skip to one side she was past him and heading for the garden door. Once through that, she'd be safe— hadn't she always thought of Bethou as a miniature castle, impenetrable from the outside? She heard him exclaim as he started after her, heard a muffled curse and a clatter as his foot slipped on a rock, then without a backward glance was through the gate and had slammed it hard. She leaned against it, panting and triumphant. By the time the tide had risen to its height and then gone down again far enough for the causeway to be exposed, her tormentor ought to be good and sick of being stranded on desert islands. And maybe then he'd go away and leave her alone!

For the next couple of hours Philippa busied herself in the house, being careful not to look out of the windows. She didn't even want to see her unwelcome visitor. She worked hard, trying to instil a more homely atmosphere into the uncared-for rooms. By the time she thought about the stranger again she had made quite a difference.

Not that she'd ever really stopped thinking about him, she admitted, looking with some satisfaction at the sitting-room, cleared of its dust-sheets now, the furniture shabby but comfortable enough, and the dining-room, its rather fine table and sideboard polished and gleaming. All the time she'd been sweeping and dusting, his face had kept forcing its way into her mind, just as he'd forced his way into her life last night and again today. The sensation that he was still on the island had been uncomfortable, to say the least; in spite of her certainty that with the garden door locked she was safe, she had also locked the house doors and put the chains up. And they were something new, she realised now with a tiny shock. Nobody had ever considered chains to be necessary on Guernsey, let alone Bethou. Was this just another indication of her father's increasingly suspicious state of mind?

All that the rooms needed now were flowers. And despite its neglect there were still plenty of those growing in the garden. Philippa went into the kitchen and hesitated at the door. Then she gave an impatient sigh. Honestly—what was she doing, was she afraid to open her own door? Was she going to let some complete stranger lay siege to her in her own house? She had the phone, didn't she? And there were weapons to hand too. . . . She glanced round irresolutely and picked up a frying-pan. No, she couldn't go out into the garden brandishing that. She looked absolutely ridiculous—and if he did happen to see her, he'd know she was scared.

Anyway, it didn't matter if he did see her. He couldn't get in. That wall was seven feet high. It had been built by a man who wanted to keep the world out and had pretty well succeeded in doing so.

Philippa opened the kitchen door and stepped outside. Some primroses would be nice, she thought, determinedly *not* looking around. And daffodils, they always cheered a room up. And perhaps a few of those—

'Oh!'

The scream died in her throat. He was there, lounging on a garden seat against the wall, looking for all the world as if he were just enjoying the sunshine. A gleam of blue slanted from between half-closed eyelids and once again there was that maddening twitch of the mobile mouth. But Philippa sensed at once that he was fully alert; the slightest move on her part back to the kitchen door and he'd be on his feet, her wrist caught once again in that iron grip. And this time he wouldn't be letting go.

'What are you doing here?' she flared, angrier than ever to find her voice cracking slightly. 'This is my *garden*! Or don't walls mean anything to you either?'

'Oh, now you didn't really mean to leave me out there all that time, did you?' he murmured. 'Okay, I was a naughty boy—but two hours is long enough, isn't it? Nearer three now. Haven't you had any lunch yet, Philippa?'

'No, I've been too busy—and the name's Miss Ozanne,' she snapped.

'Well, perhaps we can share some.' He got up and came towards her, lithe and loose-limbed as a jungle leopard. 'Look, I'm not going to hurt you. I'm just an ordinary guy. Okay, so I've teased you a little—but that's all it's been. I haven't really done anything to offend you, have I?'

Only kissed me against my will, Philippa thought, but she knew how ludicrous that would sound. She was a liberated woman, wasn't she, a product of the Eighties? She watched him doubtfully. He hadn't been so persuasive last night—he'd been brutally determined to get his own way. He had apologised this morning, saying it had been caused by fatigue and frustration, but that didn't mean he wouldn't be like it again. And she wasn't sure she wanted anyone so unpredictable in her house. He resembled that leopard in more ways than one.

'Just what are you doing here?' she asked slowly. 'It's not a coincidence that you made this the first place you've visited on Guernsey, is it? Maybe last night wasn't such a coincidence either. What's your interest in me? Why do you keep following me about—why do you keep making opportunities to be alone with me?'

The blue eyes widened for a moment, then Zane Kendrick laughed easily. 'Well, you're no dumb chick, are you?' he said admiringly. 'As a matter of fact, you're only half right, but that's not doing so badly. As it happens, last night *was* a coincidence—but you're right about today. I wanted to see you, Philippa Ozanne. I came over to see your island—but now I've seen that, it's you I want to talk to.' He let his eyes move over her, assessing her calmly while she stood gazing at him with incomprehension. 'Why don't we go inside?' he suggested reasonably. 'I've got a proposition to put to you.'

Wordlessly, Philippa led the way indoors. Whatever the stranger's proposition—and she couldn't imagine what it might be, barring the obvious—it was clear that she was going to have to put up with his presence until the tide went down, unless she chose to row him back to the main island herself. And that was a possibility; she had promised to go over and see Margaret, and she would be expected before evening. But in any case the man was obviously going to pester her until she'd heard what he had to say, so they might as well get it over with.

'Look, I wish you'd tell me what this is all about,' she said irritably, filling the kettle. 'I haven't a clue what you're doing here.'

'Sure,' he said in the amiable tone that annoyed her more than his temper the night before. 'Isn't that what I said I'd do? Isn't that why you've invited me in?'

'Oh—yes.' Now she was more confused than ever. Her hands shook a little as she spooned coffee into two mugs, and she scolded herself silently. He was only a *man*, for goodness sake! The fact that he was also standing disturbingly near, the warmth of his skin radiating rather more gently than the blast of his maleness, his breath just stirring the hair that lay close to her cheek—well, that was no reason for her hands to shake, was it? Abruptly, she turned away and opened the fridge for the milk Margaret had left there. She made coffee, found a home-made cake in the tin, and put them on the scrubbed table.

'Just what was it you wanted to talk about, Mr Kendrick?' she asked, trying to instil confidence into herself with the thought that she was on her home ground. He looked at her with amusement and stirred his coffee.

'Why not make it Zane? I've a feeling we're going to get to know each other rather well. Look, before we start, tell me one or two things about yourself. You were born here, right?'

'Yes.' Philippa's tone was guarded, but she'd told him that herself so she couldn't object.'

'But you haven't really lived here for some time——'

'Bethou's my home! It always has been.'

'Nominally, yes. But you've been at school on the mainland since you were quite a young girl, haven't you? And then college—and now you're a teacher, that right?'

Philippa stared at him. 'How do you know all this? Have you been snooping about asking questions about me? Just what's all this about anyway? I don't like——'

He lifted one hand and she floundered into silence. 'You don't like me being curious about you. Fair enough. But I did have a reason.' He paused, watching her through narrowed blue eyes. 'You see, I've been looking for a new place to live and it's struck me lately that Guernsey could be it. I like islands, I like to be near enough to the Continent to swan off for a week or two if I feel like it. I like the pace of life here, I——'

'I thought you said you'd never been here before,' Philippa cut in.

He shook his head. 'No, I don't think I ever said that.'

Philippa frowned. Maybe he hadn't *said* it—but he'd definitely left her with that impression. Anyway, she could see the way his mind was working now, though she still couldn't see why he should come to her about it.

'So?' she challenged him. 'You want to come and live

on Guernsey. I suppose that means you're rich and you
want to use it as a tax-haven. But what's it got to do
with me?'

He raised his shaggy brows. 'Surely it's obvious! I'd
like to buy your house, Philippa. I'd like to buy
Bethou.'

There was a long moment's silence. Philippa stared at
him. Her mind churned furiously. Wanted to buy
Bethou? He must be crazy—didn't he know the
situation? Didn't he realise—And then a cold anger
took the place of her chaotic thoughts. To come and
make this offer *now*, even before her father was buried!
Or maybe he just didn't know about that. Perhaps his
snooping hadn't got that far.

'I don't know if you realise, Mr Kendrick,' she said
icily, 'that my father has only just died. His funeral is
tomorrow. That's why I've come back. And I must say,
I think it's extremely insensitive of you to approach me
at such a time.'

His eyes held hers, hard as flints. 'In normal circumstances, I'd agree, Philippa. And I admit that I didn't
intend things to work out this way, but you can't
always predict your own reactions, can you? There's
something about you that makes me come right out
into the open. In any case, you're not exactly
heartbroken, are you?'

To her fury, Philippa felt her face crimson. So what if
it were true? Was it any business of *his*? Did he have
any right to point it out? And was it her fault anyway
that she couldn't feel any grief for the man who had
sent her out of his life because she reminded him too
much of her mother? Was it her fault that all she felt
was remorse, and a strange resentment that she'd never
known the love of a father?

'I think you'd better go now,' she said tightly.
'Whatever you may think, my father's death has been a
shock and I've got a lot to do. I want to go over to the
main island now to see some friends. I'll row you back
too.'

'That's fine,' he returned coolly. 'But now that I've
made the offer, you will consider it, won't you?'

'No, I won't.' Her voice was as taut as wire as she collected up the mugs, ignoring the fact that he hadn't finished his own coffee, and took them to the sink. 'And there are two very good reasons why I won't, Mr Kendrick. One is that you couldn't buy this house even if I wanted to sell it to you—it's a Local Market house, and you can only buy on the Open Market. And the other is——' and warmth flooded through her as she realised for the first time how she really felt about Bethou and about Guernsey and her future life '—the other is because I'm not selling anyway. To anyone. I'm staying here, Mr Kendrick. This is my home—and it's going to stay that way!'

It didn't take long to row across the strand. Zane Kendrick sat in the stern, his offer to row brusquely turned down by Philippa, who was feeling at last that she was in some kind of control. She was still feeling triumphant at the thought of the look on his face when she'd told him she wasn't selling—*couldn't*, as far as he was concerned. That was a stumbling-block he hadn't anticipated, and one he couldn't get over, either.

'What do you mean, I couldn't buy Bethou?' he'd asked, his brows meeting in a scowl. 'Okay, I'm pretty well off—rich by a lot of people's standards, I suppose. I could afford to live practically anywhere I want in England. Why should Bethou be out of bounds to me?'

'Because that's just what it is,' she told him triumphantly. 'Look, I'll explain. In a nutshell, when it became obvious that a lot of people were going to want to come to Guernsey because of the low taxes, the island parliament realised that unless there was some way to limit them the island would become overrun, house prices would soar and local people just wouldn't be able to afford to buy, right?'

'That's what's happened in Wales and parts of England,' he said slowly. 'People have bought cottages as holiday homes and local people can't find anywhere to live. It's caused a lot of problems.'

'Yes. Because UK governments don't have the foresight and they don't act quickly enough. In

Guernsey they use common sense. The way they found was beautifully simple. They didn't want to stop people coming in—with their high incomes, their tax is useful, even if it is so much lower than on the mainland. So they opened a register of houses and all those over a certain rateable value could qualify for what became the Open Market. They could then be sold to incomers for whatever crazy price they could fetch. Roughly, it works out at about a hundred thousand pounds more than it would be in real terms. There are some lower than that, but you can't get anything under about seventy thousand.'

'So it's a price barrier,' said Zane. 'You buy your way in and after that it's plain sailing.'

'That's right. Low income tax, no VAT, everything cheaper—it's still attractive enough to bring a lot of people here. Especially those who don't depend on being in a certain place to earn their living.' She stopped and looked at him. 'What do you do, as a matter of interest? Or have you inherited your wealth?'

'No, I work for a living, and quite hard too,' Zane told her equably. 'I'm a playwright. I've done several TV plays and a couple for the London stage. Like you say, I can work anywhere.'

'Except on Bethou,' Philippa reminded him sharply. 'Because my father never registered it for the Open Market. He hated the idea of his home going to a mainlander. And it doesn't matter how long you live here, once you're on the Open Market that's where you stay. The Local Market is strictly for the locals.'

'And the register's closed?'

She nodded. 'There haven't been any more Open Market houses for more than ten years, and I doubt if there ever will be.' She smiled at him, a smile that had more triumph in it than warmth. 'So you will have to go somewhere else to find your ideal home, Mr Kendrick. Bethou isn't for you.'

He had looked thoughtfully at her, then walked over to the window. The garden ran rampant outside, its sea of waving grasses and flowers run wild came almost up to the glass. The neglect of the past two years or more was evident in that and in the peeling paint of the kitchen door, the shabbiness of the room. He had put a finger on the windowsill and his nail had sunk into the rotting wood.

'Maybe you're right,' he had said, almost as if he were thinking of something else. 'Maybe you're right.'

But he didn't sound convinced; and when they walked out of the house and down to the beach, he had turned and looked back with an almost proprietorial air. As if, Philippa thought, seething, the whole place belonged to him already. As if it were his by *right*!

She didn't want to mention him to Hubert and Margaret when she had said goodbye to him—a real goodbye this time, she hoped—and made sure the dinghy was secure on the beach. But of course they'd seen him and were full of questions. Philippa parried their curiosity with answers as brief and noncommittal as she could make them. No, she hadn't met the man before—well, that was as nearly true as made no difference. No, he hadn't been a nuisance, not really. He was just a holidaymaker, that was all. It didn't seem necessary to tell them that he'd wanted to buy Bethou. There was no way he could, so why worry about it?

Anyway, it was too good to be with them again to let worries like that spoil their reunion. Margaret was the same as ever apart from a few extra wrinkles and grey hairs that somehow made her seem even more comfortably motherly. She welcomed Philippa as if she had indeed been her own daughter and settled her by the fire, making a fuss of her and asking a host of questions, rattling on to the next before Philippa could answer any of them. The few answers she did get seemed to satisfy her, however, and Philippa relaxed in the big chair and smiled at Hubert, who puffed his pipe on the other side of the fire.

The cottage hadn't changed at all. It was still furnished in the old Guernsey style, with a green-bed in the corner where traditionally the man of the house would rest after his midday meal. Margaret bustled about getting the meal ready and laying it on the scrubbed wooden table; spider crab, Philippa saw with delight, and bread and butter—a real Guernsey meal.

Now she knew she had really come home.

It was only later, as she rowed quietly back across the strait with the sunset turning the sky to a raging orange and the jagged rocks standing out in savage silhouette like burnt tree-stumps against the flaming backcloth, that she thought of Kevin. Was he still waiting for her to go back to him? He had never really believed that she would have the strength of mind to stay away. She had been hardly able to believe it herself. But she'd been right, she knew that as she'd known it all along. And if her pain were to be healed anywhere it must be here, far away from the strains and stresses of industrial England.

Already, she was finding Kevin's face difficult to bring to mind. When she tried, another face got in the way. A lean, dark face with glittering blue eyes and a white streak that was like a lightning flash in the night-black of his hair. . . .

## CHAPTER THREE

THE funeral next day was as simple as Philippa knew her father would have wished. In fact, she doubted if he would really have wanted a funeral at all, but tipping him over the side of a boat at sea, as he'd sometimes said was the only decent way, was out of the question, and Philippa was aware of that quirk of human psychology which demands that ceremony of some kind should attend death. Nevertheless, she walked away from the tiny churchyard with some relief that it was all over. At least she need no longer feel guilty because she couldn't even pretend to show the kind of grief that might be expected of her.

Not that anyone did seem to expect it. Everyone knew what kind of man Colin Ozanne had been, and what kind of life he had given his daughter. Few people had attended the funeral anyway—Colin had cut himself off more and more as he grew older and more of a recluse. There was Dr Edwards, who had brought Philippa into the world and suffered the shock of his career when her mother died so unexpectedly of heart failure just after the birth. There was Henry Batiste, the advocate who dealt with all her father's legal affairs. There were, of course, Tommy, with his wife Susan, and Hubert and Margaret, their faces drawn and sad as they said goodbye to a man they had known since he was a boy; and there were a few others too, who had known Philippa's father in happier days, men and women who had been at school with him and had known her mother as well.

One by one, they paid their respects and went quietly away. Philippa bent her head, feeling their sensitivity. Normally there would have been a meal after the service, with old friends and relations reminiscing over the departed. In this case, she knew that to have suggested such a thing would have been false, a pretence that her father had been different from what he was. He would not have thanked anyone for reminiscing over his life, and each person there recognised that fact.

There was another person at the funeral too. Philippa didn't notice him until she was turning away to leave the churchyard with Henry Batiste. He stood silently in the shadow of the yew tree that overhung the gate, and stepped back as she approached.

Philippa stopped short. She felt the colour drain from her face.

'What are you doing here?' she asked, her voice little more than a whisper, and Zane Kendrick inclined his head.

'It's not something I can explain right now,' he said quietly. 'But I'll come and see you in a few days, if I may.'

His last words were no more than convention, but Philippa took the chance to interpret them literally. She raised her chin, meeting the blue eyes with the chill of a moorland pool in her own.

'No, you may not,' she said. 'I don't see any purpose

in it. Don't come to Bethou, Mr Kendrick. There's nothing there for you.'

Without waiting to see the effect of her words she turned away and walked across the narrow road to Henry's car. She climbed in through the door he had already opened and sat down, aware that her face was white, just two spots of angry colour betraying her feelings. She didn't look at Zane Kendrick again, but inside she was seething with rage.

To think—just to *think*—that he'd had the colossal impudence to come to her father's funeral! And what for? He must know by now that what she'd told him about Bethou was correct, that he could never hope to buy it. So what else was he after? What could she possibly have that *still* interested him?

And why did he have this strange and frightening effect on her? Why, whenever she saw him, did her knees go weak and her palms begin to itch? Why did her heart have to thud, her colour have to change? What *was* it?

Oh, she hated him. She *hated* him!

Philippa had little appetite for her lunch with Henry Batiste, but she ate what she could and was relieved when he paid the bill and took her to his office. She didn't remember ever having been in it before; her father hadn't confided his affairs to her. But she had known Henry since she was a child and felt at ease with the kindly lawyer. She settled herself in a comfortable armchair in front of his desk and watched as he sat down behind it and sorted through some papers.

'I suppose everything was fairly straightforward, wasn't it? she said casually. 'I mean, my father had to leave the house to me, didn't he, since there are no other children. And I suppose he must have left most of the rest, too, apart from bequests to Hubert and Margaret and people like that.'

'Well, up to a point you're quite right,' Henry Batiste said, but he looked embarrassed and awkward. 'But it's not quite as simple as that, Philippa. . . . Before I go into that, however, may I ask what your own plans are?'

'My plans?' Philippa was surprised. 'Well, I hadn't really made my mind up until yesterday, but now I know I want to stay here. On Guernsey. Well——' she smiled '—on Bethou, of course.'

'You've decided that?' To her surprise he didn't look as pleased as she'd expected. Surely lawyers liked to see properties staying in the same family? 'And—er—what do you plan to do? For a living, I mean.'

'Well, I thought I'd wait to see just how much money there was. I want to put the house in order, of course, that comes first. But if I don't need to start work straightaway, I could have a long holiday—go abroad. Otherwise I suppose I'll get a job without too much difficulty, won't I?'

The advocate looked at her. He wore rimless glasses that shone when the sun came through the window and glinted on them. His face was pale, an indoor face; not very common on Guernsey, where everyone seemed to develop a tan however little time they spent out of doors. His eyes behind the glasses were an almost insipid blue.

But his mouth was kind and his expression as he looked at Philippa was compassionate. She began to feel frightened.

'My dear Philippa,' he began, and her fear grew, 'I'm afraid I have to tell you that neither of those courses is really feasible.' He coughed. 'When I asked your plans I was really hoping that you would say you intended to sell Bethou and return to the mainland. Or, if you really wanted to stay on Guernsey, to buy a smaller, more manageable house. I really did not suppose that you would want to stay there.'

'But it's my home,' Philippa began in a small voice, and he nodded.

'I know. But not quite the home you would have liked it to be, I think. I really believed that your memories of Bethou would not be of the kind you would wish to perpetuate.'

Did he realise just how many times he said 'really'? Philippa wondered irrelevantly. She tried to concentrate, to make sense of what he was saying. Did he really—oh

God, she was doing it now—did he mean that she couldn't have Bethou? That her father had left it to someone else? But he couldn't—surely—there was a law about that. The Guernsey law on inheritance was quite definite on the point—wasn't it?

'Yes, indeed,' Henry Batiste reassured her when she managed at last to voice her fear. 'Yes, Bethou is yours, as is all your father's estate, real and personal. But—well, I'm afraid there just isn't enough of it. Bethou is literally all that there is—and in real terms there isn't even that. Your father's money had come to an end, Philippa. I'm afraid all you've inherited is the island, the house—and some quite considerable debts.'

The sea glittered in the sunlight, each ripple a flash of silver. Seen from above, it was a clear, translucent green, the rocks dark shapes on the pale sandy floor. Fish darted lithely through the waving weed and on a boulder not far from the shore sat a cormorant, patiently waiting until it was time for him to dive in again to replenish his own supplies.

The cry of a tern cut through the warm air and Philippa raised her eyes to follow its swallow-like flight above the waves. Over on the clutter of rocks that formed a tiny islet off the point of Bethou she could see a group of puffins, comically solemn with their upright posture, smart black and white uniforms and huge, multi-coloured bills. They would be nesting soon, in the burrows that they dug or took over from rabbits. And on that other rock, white with the debris of centuries, the other birds would lay their eggs; guillemots, razorbills, gulls. . . .

Would she be here to see it? Could this really be her last holiday on Bethou? Was the island that had been her home, built by her grandfather, to go to strangers?

Though they wouldn't be total strangers, she comforted herself. Thanks to her father's refusal to put his house on the Open Market, Bethou could only be sold to an islander. But that was cold comfort. If he *had* registered Bethou, Philippa could at least have commanded a higher price and paid off the debts with ease. Now, it seemed that there would be barely enough after the sale ... whenever that would be. ...

'You see, Bethou is just the kind of house that really *ought* to be on the Open Market,' Mr Batiste had explained to her. 'It would appeal very much to the kind of people who choose to settle on Guernsey. But to an islander—well, the very fact that it's cut off from the main island twice a day for several hours is going to prove a handicap rather than an attraction. People who have to get to work each day aren't going to look at it, I'm afraid.'

'So I'm not going to find it easy to sell?' said Philippa, and he shook his head.

'I've very much afraid not. And you still have those debts.'

Philippa stared blindly out of the window. There was a view of the harbour; boats dancing on shimmering waters, a large ferry coming in, the smaller craft setting off for Sark or Herm. The sound of a light aircraft, familiar to all who lived or stayed on Guernsey, hummed through the opened pane. Philippa scarcely heard it.

'So that's why my father cut down Hubert and Margaret's work,' she said, half to herself. 'And I suppose that's why he didn't seem to want to see me at all, during the past few years. He didn't want me to know. ...'

Henry Batiste waited a few moments. 'Your father was a very complex man,' he said gently. 'I am sure that in his own way he loved you very deeply. Unfortunately, there was something in his make-up—some inhibition—that prevented him from showing it, except in the most oblique ways. His sending you to school, for instance——'

'Because I reminded him of my mother,' Philippa cut in swiftly.

'Exactly so. But he saw that his own pain could only harm you, and sent you away so that you might escape that—not merely so that he should be spared the sight of you. And these past few years—I know he always hoped that something would happen that would make Bethou unimportant to you. That the longer you stayed away the less likely you would be to come back—to need it, or even see it any longer as your home.'

'Yes, I can see that.' Once again Philippa was filled with pity for the lonely man who had suffered so much and understood so little. 'But it didn't work. Because I want to stay. I want to keep Bethou. It *is* my home.'

The argument had gone round and round after that. It wasn't that Henry Batiste hadn't understood or accepted her feelings; it was just that in his dry, lawyer's mind he had dismissed them as an unfortunate snag, but nothing that need stand in the way of Philippa's obvious course. Which was to sell Bethou for whatever she could get, pay off her debts and return to the mainland. Staying on Guernsey just wasn't feasible, he'd pointed out. Although unemployment wasn't as bad as on the mainland, there were only a limited number of teaching posts available, particularly as Philippa was qualified only to teach primary school children, and there was considerable competition for them. She might be lucky, but. . . . His tone left her in no doubt as to his own opinion.

Philippa had left his office with the feeling that she had suddenly become a displaced person. Until now, whatever stress and unhappiness she had endured, Bethou had always been there, at the back of her life, a stability that she had never questioned. All right, it hadn't been a particularly happy home—but it *was* home. She could always go back if she needed to, and she'd always known that one day it would belong to her.

As it now did. But in such circumstances that she couldn't possibly—according to Henry Batiste and the terrifying figures he'd shown her—keep it.

The sound of the waves, washing constantly against the foot of the low cliff, brought her back to the present. She stared unhappily at the surging sea with the seabirds constantly wheeling above it and adding their cries to the sounds that had been heard here for centuries. It would have been better, she thought bitterly, if she had never come back—never rediscovered the powerful ties that bound her to this place, the love that she would never be able to cut out of her heart now that she had found it again. It would have been better if she had simply stayed away and sent instructions for the whole place to be sold.

And even that wasn't going to be easy. It was ironic that she should have had, even before she had known the true situation, an offer to buy Bethou—an offer, moreover, from a man who seemed able to pay whatever price she asked. Even more ironical that she could not accept his offer. There was no way she could sell Bethou to Zane Kendrick—even if she wanted to— no way at all.

Philippa rose to her feet and turned her back to the waves. Since returning to Bethou after her interview with Henry Batiste, she had been concentrating on making what improvements she could to the house and garden. She hadn't actually put the house up for sale yet—she couldn't bring herself to do that straightaway—but in her heart she knew that there was really no alternative. And it would be all the better if the place looked a little less neglected; as though someone had loved and cared for it. . . .

The garden was already showing signs of improvement, she noticed with satisfaction as she went in through the garden door. She had found an old scythe and cut down quite a lot of the rank grass, and she had made a start on one of the flower-beds, which now looked a lot better with the bulk of the weeds gone and the struggling spring flowers opening their faces to the sun. It was hard work, but it was satisfying. Better, anyway, than doing nothing. She couldn't just mope about here, waiting for a sale. Neither could she leave it and return to the mainland before she absolutely had to.

Philippa went to the shed and took out a trowel and small fork. She had time to weed that second flowerbed before it began to grow dark. She knelt and began to grub among the tangle of growth, loosening roots with her fork and dragging them free to expose the dark earth. It was a pity Bethou had never been self-supporting. If there had been greenhouses here she might have been able to keep it going. But to start anything would take more capital than she had. Absorbed in her thoughts, she did not hear the knock on the garden door. Nor did she hear when it opened and Zane Kendrick put his head round. The first she knew of his presence was when he spoke.

'Well, well, well—an earth-maiden at work! Mind if I come in?'

Philippa jumped at the sound of his voice, but she knew she had been half expecting this visit. The look Zane Kendrick had given Bethou when he left it on the day before the funeral hadn't been one of farewell. She was only surprised he hadn't come sooner.

She looked up at him, resenting his cool attractiveness. If only he wouldn't smile at her in that maddening, devastating manner! If only his sapphire eyes wouldn't taunt her with their brilliance, his quirking brows mock her. . . .

Looking down at herself, she cursed silently. Once again he had her at a disadvantage—his immaculate cord suit striking a note of casual wealth that she could see suited Bethou completely. While she—Philippa closed her eyes as she acknowledged the picture she presented. Shabby jeans with mud patches on the knees, a T-shirt that really ought to have been relegated to the wash yesterday, grubby hands and, all too probably, streaks of earth across her hot face.

Rising to her feet, she said coldly: 'It seems you already have. Was there something you wanted?'

His narrowed eyes moved over her in that irritating, assessing way. 'I think you know the answer to that one, Philippa. But let's say this is just a social call—to start with, anyway. How have you been getting along?'

Philippa caught her breath. 'If there's one thing I don't like, it's insincerity, Mr Kendrick,' she told him flatly. 'You're not the slightest bit interested in how I'm getting along. You just want to get your hands on Bethou—and I'm telling you again, there's no chance. No chance at all. Unless——' She stopped suddenly and her brown eyes widened as an idea touched her mind. No—it was ridiculous. She pushed it away impatiently. 'Bethou's a Local Market house, and nothing can change that fact.'

'No, so I understand.' His look was slightly rueful. 'I've been doing my homework since I saw you last. Stupid of me not to have found out about all that before—but somehow I didn't think that was going to be a problem.' He gestured at the house. 'Could you give me a cup of coffee? I could do with one.'

Philippa sighed and led the way indoors. Why she should entertain this man she didn't know, but there seemed no other way of getting rid of him. She washed her hands at the sink and then put the kettle on. Zane sat down at the table, watching her.

Philippa felt herself colour under his scrutiny. To divert his attention she cast about for something that would interest him. And what more likely than himself? she thought cynically. Men were notorious egotists.

'What sort of plays do you write, Mr Kendrick?' she enquired. 'Adventure—police—or are you into soap opera?' She made her voice faintly scornful, as if the way he earned his money were somehow dubious.

'Comedies sometimes. But I hope I get something across in them too—some little message about life.' His tone was dry and she knew he'd caught her tone. 'And yes, I do do a few scripts for one or two of the regular series—the soap-operas, as you call them. In general, they're the most realistic of them all. Full of trivial events—just like real life. But my most recent work was a four-part serial about a homeless boy.'

'You mean *Barnaby*?' Philippa turned from the cupboard and stared at him. 'But that was good!'

His lips twitched. 'Thank you. You needn't sound quite so surprised, however.'

Philippa flushed scarlet. 'I didn't mean that—I meant——' She floundered to a stop. She couldn't say what she'd meant—that she would never have suspected this man of having the compassion, the understanding that the writer of *Barnaby* so clearly possessed. 'I'm sorry,' she finished lamely. 'I've just never met a TV writer before.'

'Oh, we're quite human.' He took the coffee she passed him and watched as she sat down opposite. 'Well, Philippa, what's the situation? Have you made up your mind to stay on Bethou?'

At once the rapport that had begun to flower, if only briefly, between them, disappeared. Philippa felt her old antagonism return in full force. What was it to do with him, after all?

'I'd rather not discuss it,' she said coldly. 'And what about you? Have you found a house you like?'

'I have, and you know which one.' Cobalt eyes met topaz across the table, and neither looked like giving way. 'Philippa, there's something you should know——'

'Are you married, Mr Kendrick?' The bald question cut into his words, taking him by surprise. His brows came together and Philippa felt his withdrawal. She'd touched a sensitive spot there, she realised, and waited with some trepidation to see what he would say next. But she had to know—it was vital to the idea that had touched her mind and now returned more insistently to nag her.

But all he said, in a curt, harsh tone, was: 'No, I'm not married. Never have been; never likely to be. Does that satisfy you?'

'Never likely to be? Why not?'

'Because I don't choose to be,' he snapped. 'And before you get the wrong idea, I'm completely normal—that's been proved over and over. I just don't happen to be all dewy-eyed over romance and the idea that there's just one woman for every man.'

'Maybe you don't really like women at all,' Philippa suggested. 'Maybe you just like using them.'

'Maybe I do.' His eyes were like chips of flint now and Philippa guessed that he'd been hurt at some time by some woman, and hurt badly. Only he didn't mean to show the bruises.

Well, that was all right. She could understand it—didn't she feel the same way herself? Philippa had never confided in anyone about Kevin. But the pain of giving him up was still very much there and she was convinced she would never love another man.

'So you wouldn't consider marriage?' She stirred her coffee, keeping her eyes down. 'Not at any price?'

'What sort of price?' His tone was guarded. 'And who's doing the paying?'

Philippa took a deep breath. It was now or never. The idea that had come unbidden to her mind was incredible—fantastic—outrageous. But it could just work—between two people who didn't love each other but were each set against loving anyone else. Just as well as between two who *did* love; and she pushed that thought away, with all the bleak loneliness it brought with it.

'My father died a poor man,' she said quietly. 'He left me Bethou and a string of debts. I can't pay the debts until I've sold the house and I'm not going to find it easy to sell the house. Because of its position, it would be more attractive on the Open Market than it is on the Local, and I can't do a thing about that. I can't sell it to you, even though I know you want it—but there is one way you could have it.'

'And that is?' He was very still now, watching her, and Philippa knew that he was well aware of what he was about to say, but still wanted to hear it. She took another breath and wondered if she'd gone stark raving mad.

'You could marry me,' she said. 'Marry me and pay off the debts. Then we would both have the house. The price would be that we'd have each other too.'

The silence this time was a long one. Philippa could see the idea moving around in Zane Kendrick's brain. There was something else there too—something she didn't quite understand. Maybe it had to do with a woman. But he hadn't turned her down outright. He was thinking about it.

She was still having to think about it herself. The idea had come to her only moments ago. It was a crazy, impulsive idea and up to now all her crazy, impulsive ideas had led to trouble. The kind of trouble this one could lead to would put all those others completely in the shade. But whatever happened, she would have Bethou. She would still have her home. And during the past week or so she had come to realise more and more just how important this was to her.

'Let's get this quite clear,' Zane said at last. 'You're suggesting we get married, so we both have the house. I pay off the debts and we live here together, right?'

'Yes.' Philippa's voice was husky. It sounded crazy—why didn't he *say* it was crazy? Her heart was hammering inside her ribcage. By now, she wasn't even sure whether she wanted him to say yes or no.

'Presumably you'd expect me, as your husband, to keep you as well.'

The dryness in his tone brought a blush to Philippa's cheeks. She hadn't even thought of that! And if she said yes, what else would it imply? She looked up and caught the searing glance, and looked away hastily. This was another problem—the intensely disturbing effect his physical presence had on her. But she would overcome that, when she was seeing more of him, surely?

'I'll get a job,' she said quickly. 'I'm a qualified teacher, but I could work in an office or a shop, or anything. I don't mean to be a burden to you.'

'Oh no,' he said at once, 'that wouldn't do. I'm the old-fashioned type. My wife doesn't work.'

Philippa felt helpless. She began to wonder if she was getting into some kind of a trap. But what other way was there? It was either this or return to the mainland, and she knew now that she just couldn't do that.

'There's a lot to be sorted out,' he went on thoughtfully. 'But it could work. Marriages of convenience have happened before—quite a few cultures swear by them still. And marriages for love don't seem to have to much to crow over.'

The edge in his voice brought her eyes to his face again, but there was nothing in his expression to give him away. Clearly, he *had* been hurt—and, just as clearly, he didn't intend to say anything about it. Well, she wasn't going to mention Kevin either, so that was fair enough.

'There's a lot needs doing to the house,' he continued. 'It wouldn't end with just paying your debts. And you'd expect me to go on maintaining it, too.'

'You would if you bought it,' Philippa reminded him quickly, and he inclined his head.

'True. So you can say that it's just the debts. What do they amount to?'

Philippa told him and he whistled softly. 'He certainly left you with a load of trouble, your father. What the hell had he been doing with it all?'

Philippa shrugged. 'Just living on it. Sending me to school must have drained his resources. He was living on borrowed money for years. I suppose he thought I'd just sell Bethou and break a little more than even. That's why he didn't encourage me to come here. He wanted me to forget it.'

'But you didn't.' The dark blue eyes rested on her face. 'You put it out of your mind—but you never really forgot it, is that right?'

'Yes, that's right.' Philippa's voice was low. She looked beseechingly across the table at him. 'Have—you decided, Mr Kendrick? Will you think about my suggestion? Or is it all so crazy that you won't even consider it?'

'Oh, I'll consider it. It's certainly worth that, if nothing else. But like I said, there are a lot of things to sort out first. This being one of them.'

He stood up and came round the table towards her. Philippa watched with wide amber eyes as his big, loose-limbed body moved with easy grace, coming closer every moment. She wanted to get up and run, but she couldn't move; she was riveted to her chair, hypnotised by the piercing blue eyes. Her heart was making huge, rhythmic jumps in her breast, her throat felt choked and her palms tingled. She felt the two big hands grasp her arms, just above the elbow; tensed as they drew her up out of the chair, their grip one that she couldn't resist; felt the big, lean body against hers, the muscles hard against her softness. She wanted to protest, raised her head and opened her mouth to do so, then gasped as the firm lips met hers, cutting off all possibility of speech as they moved with a practised ease that had her whimpering in his arms.

Her senses reeled. She felt her own arms slip up his

back, clinging to him, her fingers moving against his shoulder-blades, and she heard him give a tiny grunt of satisfaction. Then he had lifted her in his arms and as she turned her face against his shoulder she felt him kick open the door that led to the sitting-room. The sound of the waves outside washed into her consciousness as Zane laid her on the sofa and knelt beside her; she opened eyes that had darkened to the colour of mahogany to gaze at him, taking in every detail of his craggy face, the bristling brows, the brilliant eyes, the chiselled lips. He gave a muttered exclamation and kissed her again, blotting out all thought as his mouth plundered hers, taking and tasting, compelling a response that she had never suspected was within her. His long fingers slid down her neck and fumbled with the buttons of the loose shirt she wore over her jeans so that it fell away, leaving her breasts revealed in the wisp of lace that passed for a bra, and with a swift movement he wrenched it aside and exposed the rosy curves.

Philippa gasped as his fingers touched her breasts, caressing them and moulding them, then closed her eyes as his lips left her mouth to travel burningly down to take one nipple tenderly between firm teeth. She moved convulsively in his arms, holding his head close to her, twisting sinuously against him in her need to get even closer. She had never, never experienced anything like this before. Even with Kevin——

*Kevin!* With a violent wriggle, she was out of Zane's arms and crouched in a corner of the sofa, staring with wide eyes as he shook his head dazedly and gazed at her in astonishment. She was supposed to be in love with Kevin, wasn't she? Even if she'd given him up—what kind of a girl was she, that she could behave like this with a man she hardly knew?

'What in hell's name——' Zane began, but Philippa had some kind of control now and she snapped back at him, taking the offensive in a desperate bid to regain her self-respect.

'Let's get this clear, Mr Kendrick! This marriage—if it happens—is just what you said it was—a marriage of convenience. Not free access for a spot of sex whenever you feel like it. That goes with love in my book—and I think you said that love was out, didn't you? You don't believe in it, right? So no more kisses, is that clear? Or anything—anything at all!'

She panted into silence, keeping her blazing eyes fixed on the angry face before her. She didn't expect him to accept her conditions at once—he'd shown all too clearly what kind of a man he was—but unless he did there was no deal, and he'd better understand it!

Zane passed a hand across his chin, then rubbed it up over his face. His scowl faded, leaving his expression inscrutable. Philippa quailed. She had seen that expression—or non-expression—before and it boded ill. But he couldn't force her, she reminded herself bravely. She still held the trump card—Bethou. If he wanted the house, he wouldn't take any chances.

'Funny,' he said at last, and his voice was as easy and noncommittal as if she had refused him an apple. 'I thought you were as keen as I was for a few moments there. Must have been mistaken—though I can usually tell.' He glinted a look at her. 'Sure you don't want me to go on? OK, OK, don't get worked up about it.' He got to his feet, brushing his well-cut cords down absently. 'So sex is out, is it? Well, I guess I'll live. And you never know, you may change your mind. Right, Philippa, it's a deal. We get married, on your terms— and we share Bethou. That's it, isn't it?'

Philippa looked at him suspiciously. She hadn't expected him to give in this easily. It just proved how right she'd been to put a stop to it, though. Zane Kendrick was obviously the kind of man who took his fun lightly, where and when he found it. He would have enjoyed his romp with her—enjoyed many more, presumably, when they were married—but it would never have meant anything to him. To him, it would have been lust, easily satisfied. Never love.

She supposed that he was comforting himself with the idea that he would continue life as before, with women friends who shared the same views, and the thought gave her an odd twinge of discomfort. Still, she couldn't

have it all ways. And it was Bethou that mattered—
mattered to them both.

For the first time, she wondered just why it mattered
so much to Zane Kendrick. Why he wanted it so much
that he was prepared to marry a girl he didn't love to
get it.

She didn't get the chance to ask him. He stood up,
smoothed down his thick black hair and glanced out of
the window.

'Tide's on the turn,' he remarked laconically. 'I'd
better be going. Don't want to be stuck here all night—
not just yet.'

He turned as Philippa scrambled out of the sofa and
stood, slim and still trembling slightly, in the middle of
the room. 'I'll be over again tomorrow,' he said easily,
as if they had just been enjoying afternoon tea together.
'We've quite a few arrangements to make.' He reached
out a finger and trailed it down Philippa's cheek and
into the neck of her shirt. 'Don't worry—I've taken
your point. No sex—at least, until *you* say so. And you
never know—that may not be so very long!' He gave
her a quick, flashing grin and strode lightly from the
room.

Philippa stood where he had left her. Her hands were
clenched into fists, her teeth bit into her lip until she
tasted blood. What in God's name did he think he
meant? What did he think she was? No sex, she'd said,
and that was what she *meant*. And it didn't matter how
much her body longed to give in—how much it cried
out for his kisses and his caresses—she wasn't going to
change her mind. Never. Never! *Never!*

## CHAPTER FOUR

PHILIPPA's wedding day dawned with a storm. She got
out of bed and looked resignedly out of the window,
watching the waves as they foamed violently against the
rocks, smothering the higher crags with boiling curds,

then falling back into the surging grey-green depths before making a second assault. The wind roared round the isolated house like a pack of starving wolves, as it had done all night, keeping Philippa awake and wide-eyed in her big bed. Tomorrow night she would no longer be alone in the house, she had thought, and wondered just what it would be like to live with Zane— or at least, to share her home with him. Living together sounded altogether much more intimate than she was, even now, prepared for.

During the weeks that had had to elapse before they could get married she and Zane had spent a good deal of time together, getting to know each other, yet she still felt that he was a stranger, that she was groping her way towards understanding and had little hope of reaching it. She felt that there were parts of him that he kept hidden from her. Perhaps that was true of any couple, especially where the man was several years older—Zane was thirty-eight, sixteen years older than Philippa—but she had a feeling that those hidden facets were parts that she needed to know, parts that were important to her—to them both. But Zane wasn't the kind of man you could draw secrets from, she'd discovered. What he didn't want to tell remained concealed, buried deep in the complexities of his nature.

Apart from the mystery that still surrounded him— who and where were his family, for example, and just why did he want Bethou so badly—Philippa had been relieved to find that they could get along together quite well, even enjoy each other's company. They had walked all over the island together, exploring the leafy lanes, the dizzying cliff paths and the broad sands. They had borrowed Hubert's boat and gone fishing, bringing their spoils back to cook for supper. They had sauntered around the harbour of St Peter Port, admiring the variety of yachts that were moored there and picking out the ones they liked best.

'I might buy a boat,' Zane said thoughtfully, leaning over the rails to gaze at a particularly seaworthy-looking vessel. 'Haven't had much chance to sail a lot lately, but it would be a good thing to do here. We could slip over to France. . . . Have you done a lot of sailing, Philippa?'

'I used to,' she said dreamily, thinking of the days she'd spent at sea, first with Hubert and then with various friends who had taken her out during her school holidays. 'It would be nice to take it up again.'

'Then perhaps we will,' he promised, turning away to inspect a small ketch that was just entering harbour. 'We make quite a good team in a boat.'

For some unaccountable reason his words gave Philippa a pang. Was that all he saw in her? A good team-mate in a boat? But they were going to be *married*!

She caught herself up sharply at that thought. What was she thinking of? This was a marriage of convenience, convenience to them both. Not the kind of marriage she had envisaged during her schooldays; not the kind of marriage she might have had with Kevin, if things had been different. But the only kind left to her now, now that she could never have love.

A good team-mate, whether in a boat or anywhere else, was just about all she could expect. It was better than she had anticipated when she had first suggested this arrangement. So there was no reason—no reason at all—for her to watch Zane with hungry eyes, wonderin what it would be like to be loved by him—to love him in return. Those were questions that would never be answered, and it was better not even to ask them.

Zane didn't touch her again during their strange courtship. He was careful not to brush against her as they walked and if he passed her something at table he always set it down quickly so that her fingertips would not touch his. Philippa found herself conscious of an irritation that made her want to beat him at this game—force him, somehow, to touch her. She was half glad and half angry that her tactics never succeeded—there was no knowing, after all, what such a touch might lead to. The tension between them was electric, and the slightest spark could cause an explosion.

She was conscious too of the mockery in Zane's eyes when she had deliberately stumbled so that he would

have to steady her—removing his hand the moment she
had regained balance—or let her fingers linger on the
salt-cellar as he was about to take it. He clearly knew
quite well what she was doing; the humiliation made
her cheeks burn and she would vow not to submit to
the temptation again. But she always did, and as time
went on the urge became more and more powerful. It
kept her awake at night; woke her from dreams that he
was with her, his lips on hers, his fingertips blazing fire
through her body, his arms enclosing her in a world
whose existence she barely understood.

And now the last night was over. Today they were to
be married, tonight he would be here in the house with
her. And then . . .?

Restlessly, Philippa turned away from the window
with its panoramic view of Guernsey and the furious
tide that surged across the strait between it and Bethou.
She went into the adjoining bedroom. She was still not
completely sure of Zane's intentions. Did he mean to
consummate their marriage, to make her his wife in
reality? Her heart kicked at the thought. It hadn't been
*her* intention—she was still determined to remain loyal
to Kevin—but would she actually be able to prevent
him? She would say no, of course, tell him that the
marriage was for convenience only—but what if he
ignored her wishes? She had experienced enough in his
arms to know that if he began to kiss her, to make love
to her, she would be unable to resist. There was a
chemistry between them that couldn't be denied, an
instinct as old as humanity itself that clamoured to be
fulfilled. A shiver ran over her body as she stood at the
bedroom door. *Surely* he wouldn't insist, knowing that
there was no love between them . . . *surely.* . . .

The room had been furnished with some care and
Philippa had decided to make it her wedding-present to
Zane. Secretly, making sure that he knew nothing of it,
she had chosen strong, masculine-looking furniture that
suited the solid house. Rich brown carpet rippled across
the floor and deep gold velvet curtains framed the
windows. She was especially pleased with the bedspread,
a jungle print of browns and golds in a thick fur fabric

that seemed to her to epitomise all the unleashed wildness that she sensed in Zane's character, the hidden power of the basking leopard, the implicit strength of the pacing tiger.

She had better begin to get ready. The wedding was timed for twelve o'clock and then there was to be a lunch at one of the island's best hotels, with both Hubert and Tommy, together with Margaret and Susan present, as well as Henry Batiste and his wife. There were to be no other guests; Philippa hadn't wanted any of her old friends to witness what she still considered to be a farce, a way of keeping Bethou and nothing else. Not that even the Batistes or the Fallas realised that. They had been surprised at the sudden engagement, even shocked, but she had told nobody the real reason for it. And she suspected that, having recovered from their original astonishment, they had even been pleased that she was to settle down to married life on Bethou.

'That needs to be a real family home,' Margaret had said, her wrinkled face beaming with approval. 'Something it's never really been, somehow. You'll open it up to life, Miss Philippa, make it what it ought to be. Fill it up with little 'uns, that's what's needed.'

And just what it won't get, Philippa thought with a stab of uncertainty. *Was* she doing the right thing? Wasn't she just perpetuating the sadness of the house by this marriage—this marriage without a heart? Well, time alone would tell. She must just do her best. But a loneliness crept into her heart at the thought of those children who would never be, the family Bethou had waited for and would still never know.

If the wedding-day hadn't been so soon, Philippa might even then have changed her mind. But there was so much to do—and Zane, taking up so much of her time, was so gentle and considerate that her first impressions of him began to fade—that it was upon her before her half-formed doubts could resolve themselves. And now it was here, and the weather itself seemed determined to keep her on Bethou. She wondered what would happen if she just couldn't get across the strait— but the tide would be down by then and Hubert would be over to fetch her.

It wasn't every bride who set out for her wedding on a tractor, she thought half-hysterically as she ran a bath and sank into the hot, scented water. Tommy's best taxi would be waiting on the other side, of course, but she'd still had to choose her clothes with an eye to the possibility of getting drenched on the way. Though if the worst came to the worst, she could always change in Margaret's cottage.

As it happened, there was no need. By ten-thirty the wind had dropped and the skies were clearing. And as Philippa brushed her dark cap of hair and slipped into the cream lace dress she had bought in the island's best boutique, she knew that the sun would, after all, be shining on her for her wedding-day. Whatever that might mean.

She took a final look at herself in the mirror as she saw Hubert setting out from the other side with the tractor. She had lost weight in the past weeks; her figure was more slender than ever, though its curves were just as pretty, and her face was pale, her eyes large and dark. Not very bridal, she thought ruefully; the dress, though of cream lace, wasn't long and flowing but short and simply cut. Almost stark, she thought now, though it had looked just right in the shop. Well, it would have to do. She wasn't planning to knock Zane's eye out, after all. She was only *marrying* him!

In spite of her doubts, Hubert's eyes widened with appreciation when she came out of the house to greet him. He cleared his throat and brushed a hand across his eyes as he took her hand and Philippa looked at him in surprise. She had been so concerned with her own doubts and worries that she had forgotten that to Hubert and Margaret this was a normal wedding-day, a joyous occasion. He saw her as a true bride; more than that, he saw Bethou continuing in her and Zane's hands, becoming the happy home it had never quite been, filled with their children, vibrant with love and laughter. He saw his own life still bound up with hers, the Fallas and the Ozannes going on together as they had done for generations; and her eyes blurred with emotion and a strange sadness that all was not as

Hubert thought it. She felt that she was deceiving this old man who had shown her nothing but kindness since her childhood, deceiving him and his motherly wife, and she felt a wash of shame as she held the wrinkled hand and smiled into the old eyes.

'A real little bride you look,' he was saying softly, holding her hand in both of his. 'A real, old-fashioned little bride. . . . I'm glad I'm here to see the day, Miss Philippa.'

Philippa climbed up beside him in the tractor and they lumbered across the causeway to where Margaret and Tommy waited at the road's end on the low cliff. Again, Philippa was conscious of the sentimental pleasure in their eyes as they gazed at her and Margaret folded her arms around her for a kiss. Much more of this and she would have to call the whole thing off, she thought in dismay. Somehow it had never occurred to her that what she had looked on as a private arrangement between herself and Zane could affect other people so strongly. She felt as if she were taking part in some mad charade that couldn't be stopped. It was the first time in her life that she had practised deceit, and she felt ashamed and unhappy. True, the arrangement was plain enough between her and the man she was about to marry—and she'd supposed that that was enough. But it clearly wasn't. And by now she was in too deeply to draw back. The deceit would still be there even if she put a stop to the whole thing at this very moment. Hubert, Margaret and Tommy would know what she had done. And she would lose Bethou.

No, there was nothing for it but to go ahead. Zane would be waiting at the register office—and in spite of her worries a tiny thrill ran down her spine at the thought. And in any case, she couldn't imagine him allowing her to pull out now—the violence that she still sensed lurking beneath that relaxed façade shown during their brief engagement would be unleashed in all its fury, and she just couldn't cope with that.

Tommy ushered them all into the car and Philippa sat in the back with Margaret, trying to relax. The older woman smiled at her twisting fingers and produced a small posy of spring flowers which she laid in Philippa's lap. 'A bouquet for a bride, my dear,' she murmured. 'Don't tear it to bits before we get there. . . . I still think it's a pity you're not having a church wedding. It never seems quite finished to me, that register office thing.'

'Zane didn't want it,' Philippa told her, repeating the story they'd agreed on. 'He wasn't brought up in that church.' True enough, though he hadn't told her which religion, if any, he did profess to; but the real reason had been Philippa's dislike of using the church for what was, after all, a loveless arrangement. Zane had been quite willing to be married in church—had even, she thought in some surprise, seemed a little disappointed at her refusal. Philippa herself had been disappointed that she was being denied a church wedding, but she knew that she could not have stood at the altar and repeated words that her heart was denying.

Yet again she thought of Kevin. If only it could have been he that waited for her this morning! But even as she thought it the words rang hollow in her mind and Kevin's image was faint. Perhaps marriage with him never had been a possibility; certainly it had become unthinkable once there was a chance of his wife returning to him. She wondered what he was doing now, what he would think if he knew what was happening here on Guernsey. True to her vow, she hadn't contacted him at all since she'd left, and she had never given him her address. It had had to be a clean break.

The taxi turned a last corner and glided down the steep, narrow road into St Peter Port. The Town Church stood square and solid in the centre, boats danced in the glittering harbour where only a faint reminder of the wind that had tossed them through the night now blew white flecks off the choppy waves. People thronged the little streets; holidaymakers, more every week as the summer drew nearer, browsed among the shops. It was Thursday and in the afternoon the traditional Guernsey Market would take place in the Market Square, the stallholders arrayed in local costume to sell such wares as handknitted guernseys,

candles, woodcarvings and pottery; there might even be
dancing between the gaily-striped awnings of the stalls,
and everyone would be in a mood for celebration.

Everyone except me, Philippa thought as she entered
the register office with a sinking heart. Because I won't
be celebrating the start of a new life—I'll be saying
goodbye to an old one, with all its promise. I'll be
bending myself to a future that is impossible to
envisage, with a man I hardly know.

Panic rose in her throat at the thought and she
stopped, half inclined to turn and run; but before her
pause could even be remarked on, a tall shadow
detached itself from a doorway and with a sense of
inevitability she recognised Zane, immaculate in a grey
suit that emphasised the breadth of his shoulders, the
narrowness of his waist and the long, lean length of his
thighs. His eyes glimmered like stars in the darkness of
the building, dim after the bright sunshine outside, and
he looked grave as he reached out both his hands and
drew Philippa towards him.

'That rarity, a bride who arrives on time,' he said,
and bent to kiss her. Philippa felt a twinge of
excitement in her stomach. It was the first time he had
kissed her since the day they had agreed to marry, and
although it was quite passionless it nevertheless
disturbed her deeply. She trembled under his hands and
he drew back and gave her a quizzical glance.

'Not too nervous, are you?' he asked softly, and she
shook her head. It was just an *arrangement*, she told
herself desperately. A few words, a signature, a piece of
paper—that was all. A business contract—call it what
you liked. Nothing to feel nervous about. No reason—no
reason at all—why she should feel so tremulous, like a
real bride; no reason why her eyes should mist with
tears at this gentle kiss from her groom.

It seemed only moments before they were out again in
the sunshine. Philippa stared about her, dazed and
bewildered. The streets were just as busy, the people
just as bustling as they had been before she went in. It
was as if nothing had changed—yet it had. For her, the

whole world had changed. Yet nobody seemed to know. Nobody seemed to care.

It wasn't merely the effect of being married; the strange sensation of having been at one moment single, at the next bound for life to the tall, grave-faced man beside her. That had been shattering enough. But to discover, almost immediately afterwards, that he wasn't the man she had thought ... that there was a mystery she hadn't begun to divine—that had shaken her badly. A tumult of emotion had drowned her shy nervousness; she felt bewilderment, anger and a sick apprehension. Why hadn't he told her? Why had he hidden the truth about himself—whatever it was? What did it mean?

She felt Zane's hand under her elbow and fear jolted through her; she wanted to push him away, turn and run, get out of his life. But that was the one thing she couldn't do, because in those few minutes she had become his wife and nothing would ever be the same again.

'Tommy's just bringing the car,' Zane said in her ear, his breath warm and sweet on her cheek. 'I've booked a table at the O.G.H.; we'll celebrate in style. You look very lovely, Philippa.'

Philippa turned and looked up at him. Confused topaz eyes searched cool, enigmatic blue. She shook her head, trying to clear the muddled thoughts that churned through her mind, and her hair flicked into dark feathers around her brow. Most of all, she knew she needed to be alone, to talk to Zane, to find out the truth behind the shock he had just dealt her the moment they were married; a shock she hoped none of the others had noticed, putting her trembling hand down to the natural nervousness of a bride signing her maiden name for the last time. But there was no chance for them to be alone; the others were gathered round them, laughing and talking, insisting on photographs being taken. She stood with a face like marble, her hand in Zane's arm, while they had their way, then climbed gratefully into Tommy's taxi, polished and beribboned for the occasion. Zane was beside her, his grey suit touching her cream lace; she could feel the warmth and strength of his body against hers and she tried to shrink away, but there wasn't room. His hand found hers, and she wished desperately that she could find it reassuring rather than a threat. Then they were moving, finding a way through the sauntering crowds up the street to the Old Government House Hotel, perched almost at the highest point of the town, where Henry and Jacqueline Batiste were already waiting for them.

To a casual onlooker the lunch party must have seemed just like any other small celebration; a group of friends laughing and toasting each other in champagne, the smiling waiters scurrying round to give them the best service that could be offered. They sat by the wide windows at the end of the banqueting hall, surrounded by the grandeur of a past age—gold panelled walls, crystal chandeliers, heavy drapes, all the elegance of the Regency style of décor. From the window they looked out over the small, secluded swimming-pool beyond the terrace, and across the rooftops to the harbour. Philippa gazed out across the sea at the shadowy outlines of Guernsey's neighbouring islands, Herm and Sark, and wondered just what she was doing here.

She ate her meal almost mechanically. The O.G.H., as it was affectionately called, was well known for its food and at any other time she would have enjoyed it. But today—today, when she had not only married a man she did not love, but had made a discovery immediately after that marriage that had shaken her to her roots— she might as well have been eating ashes. The first two courses, of avocado followed by soup, she scarcely noticed; the main course of lobster she could not finish; and when the laden sweet trolley arrived with its burden of delicious temptation, she shook her head and would only accept a small piece of cheese.

Why—*why*? What did it mean? She didn't even know her own name—she didn't know whether she was now legally Philippa Kendrick, or still Philippa Ozanne. She looked at Zane, sitting beside her, unable to comprehend the meaning of what she had seen. Why couldn't he at least have told her—warned her? Instead of which, he had just left her to find out, in the cruellest way possible. And she wasn't even sure what she *had* found out. But it was obviously something he hadn't intended her to know; that much had been made clear by his own hesitation when he had come to sign the register.

Philippa's mind went back again to that moment, when the words of the marriage ceremony were over and the registrar had produced his heavy book for them to sign. They had each quickly scanned the certificate to make sure that everything was correct, and then they had, in turn, put their signatures at the bottom.

Philippa Mary Ozanne. And Zane Kendrick Ozanne.

*Ozanne.* His name was the same as hers. He too hailed, at some point, from Guernsey, where that name was so common. And he had never told her.

*Why?*

It seemed an eternity before they were able to say goodbye to their guests and return to Bethou, and in that time Philippa had no opportunity to speak privately with Zane. She caught his glance several times and knew that he was aware of her feelings, but there was nothing to be read in that inscrutable expression; certainly no hint of apology. At that thought, she seethed with anger. Just what was he playing at? What was behind this deception of his?

Her eyes turned to Henry Batiste, who had signed the register as witness, together with his wife. Had they known? Did they know Zane's true background? And if so, why hadn't they told her? Henry was her advocate, wasn't he? It was his duty to look after her affairs. Why had he allowed this deception to go ahead? Why hadn't he warned her?

She had to admit that he had tried. When she had first told him of her engagement he had looked first surprised, then wary. He had asked her whether she had really given it enough thought, so soon after her father's death, asked her just how much she knew about this stranger, famous as a playwright though he might be, and Philippa had virtually snapped his head off. All too conscious of the fact that her reasons for the marriage—for actually *proposing* marriage to Zane—

might not bear scrutiny, she had taken refuge in a defensive hostility. Yes, of course she'd given it sufficient thought. Yes, of course she knew Zane well enough. And Henry had sighed and said no more.

The final good wishes over, Philippa climbed into Zane's car. He had returned the Renault he had hired to the garage and bought himself a new Saab, sleek and luxurious, with seats that seemed to enfold the body like comfortable armchairs. It was a soft blue, with upholstery to match, and Philippa leaned back her head and closed her eyes for a moment. It would be good just to fall asleep now—to wake up and find that all this had been some strange, vivid dream and that she was back in Coventry, teaching her class of infants, or even just arriving at Bethou with no knowledge of what was to come. But no—for then she had to live through it all again. And it was no use telling herself that she wouldn't make the same mistakes—Philippa knew that if the circumstances were repeated she would do exactly the same, for there would still be no other course open to her.

She was scarcely aware of the journey across the island and it seemed that all too soon they were at the garage close to Hubert's cottage where Zane was to keep his car. It had always belonged to Bethou, though Colin Ozanne had never bothered with a car, relying on Tommy's taxi for the few journeys he had to make. Philippa got out and waited while he put the car away. She glanced ruefully at her fine, strappy sandals. The causeway was dry enough to cross, which meant it was as wet as a country path after a heavy storm; stretches of water gleamed along it and although they were only an inch or two deep they wouldn't do her sandals much good, and she had forgotten to bring anything stronger.

'It's all right,' said Zane, reading her thoughts. 'Hubert said I could use the tractor. I'll run it back after I've changed my own clothes.'

'Can you drive a tractor?' Philippa asked, following him down to the beach. Her question was little more than mechanical; she was all too well aware that for all the time they had spent together in the past weeks she

still knew very little about him. He might have been a
lion-tamer for all she knew, and certainly one glance
from those flint-hard eyes could have quelled most wild
animals!

'Oh yes,' he answered her casually. 'I was brought up
on a farm, I can turn my hand to most things.'

A farm! Philippa shook her head as she scrambled up
beside him. Anyone less like a farmer's son. . . . But it
had probably been some large country estate rather
than the kind of farm she knew; most likely his father
had been some absentee landowner and Zane had spent
his holidays there, doing whatever he fancied and using
the place as a kind of vast playground. . . .

But then where did his name fit in? That Ozanne that
had come after the Kendrick which was in fact his
middle name? That was a Guernsey name, there was no
getting away from it, and until she understood why he
held it and why he hadn't told her, her mind would
continue to go round in these dizzying circles. . . .

Neither spoke during the short journey. They
disembarked from the tractor and walked up the shore.
Philippa's heart was beating fast. This was where their
marriage—such as it was—would truly begin. This was
the moment when she would cease to be the sole owner
of Bethou, her family home, and begin to share it with
her husband—a stranger. She hesitated and looked up
at the granite walls. They had held so much
unhappiness and bitterness in the past. What was to be
their future? Had she done the right thing? Or was she
to regret it—was she condemning herself to a future as
lonely and as bitter as her father's?

'Let's go in,' Zane said quietly, and Philippa took a
grip on herself. What was the matter with her—she'd
asked for this, hadn't she? She'd proposed to Zane—
she'd used his wealth and his desire to own Bethou, to
get what *she* wanted. So wasn't it fair that she accepted
the situation as it was?

Yes—it was. Except for that one deception—the
deception that changed everything, turned the whole
thing upside down. . . .

Together, they went through the garden door. It

looked very different inside from the way it had been when Philippa had come home such a short time ago. Her own early efforts on the garden had been supplemented by Hubert, restored to working full-time on Bethou, and Zane himself, who had proved to be a tireless pioneer in the jungle that Bethou's garden had become. Rampant shrubs had been tamed, weeds destroyed and the lawns and flowerbeds re-established. Hubert's vegetable plot was now smoothly raked and planted, and the raspberry canes and strawberry beds brought back under control.

As far as Bethou itself was concerned, Philippa thought, she had definitely done the right thing. Already the house had a subtly changed air, an air of being loved and cared for, even though little had yet been done to it apart from the garden. Zane had been keen to get the renovations and redecorations done as soon as possible, but Philippa had taken charge there. She wanted to get that bedroom finished before the wedding—after that, he could do what he liked. And so Clive, Hubert's nephew, had come over every day with his paints and his papers, and Zane had not been allowed to see what he was doing.

And now the moment had come. Zane had come to Bethou, not as a visitor but as its owner. Or part-owner—Henry Batiste had already drawn up the documents and wills that made them joint owners of all their possessions, thus avoiding the complications that could arise under Guernsey's inheritance laws. Philippa's hand trembled a little on the door-handle. From now on he could come and go as he pleased—go where he liked in the house, do as he wanted there. He was her husband, she was his wife. How was it going to work out?

'Come in,' she said in a deep breath. 'I don't know about you, but I'm dying for a cup of tea. And Margaret's given us a fresh Guernsey *gache*. Would you like some?'

Oh God, she sounded like some bright little housewife inviting a neighbour in! But Zane only smiled at her and said quietly: 'I never refuse Margaret's *gache*, Philippa. But do you mind if I take my things upstairs first? I had them brought over while we were at lunch and they're stacked just outside the door.'

'Your—things? Oh yes, of course.' This was *stupid*, she thought half-hysterically. Why couldn't she act naturally, for heaven's sake? But her palms were tingling and the sensation was spreading right up her arms and into her chest, making breathing difficult. Her legs were threatening to give way too if she didn't sit down, and her heart was beating high in her throat. For goodness' sake calm down, she scolded herself. You've been here with Zane before—he's never touched you, since that day. . . . But things were different now. They were married, and he was standing disturbingly close, that magnetic aura emanating from him with an almost tangible force that hit her like a blow to the heart. 'Yes,' she repeated, grabbing at the chance to get away from him, if only for a few minutes to pull herself together, 'you take them upstairs and I'll make the tea. I'll take it into the sitting room, all right?'

Without waiting to see his response she escaped into the kitchen and leaned back against the door, eyes closed, fighting to overcome the weakness that had invaded her. If only he weren't so *attractive*! For a moment she longed for Kevin. All right, she was married now—but that needn't stop her loving him, need it? He had come first into her heart—and this marriage *was* only for convenience. Just let her remember that—it was the only way to keep control. . . .

She was just pouring out the tea when Zane came back into the kitchen, and now he was no longer smiling. With a glance of alarm, Philippa saw that his mood seemed to have changed completely; his air of quiet reassurance had vanished and in its place was a suppressed fury that filled the kitchen with shock waves and had her back against the sink, kettle in hand almost as a weapon, gazing at him with wide brown eyes.

'Zane?' she began in a whisper, but he cut in ruthlessly, his tones hard and arrogant.

'All right, Philippa, let's have it. Just what are you

playing at?' He was breathing quickly, his black brows drawn together in a solid, shaggy bar across his ice-hard eyes. 'What's the idea of decorating my bedroom that way? I take it it *is* my bedroom—not *ours?*'

The meaning in his words was unmistakable and Philippa felt her cheeks flush. 'Yes, you're right, it *is* your bedroom,' she retorted, unable to understand the reason for his anger but ready to retaliate. 'I had it decorated for your wedding-present. What's wrong with it? Don't you like it?'

'*Like* it?' he echoed, and she wondered again why, even if he hated it, he had to be quite so angry. '*Like* it—that doesn't come into it. I just want to know what you had in mind when you chose the décor. Just what you're trying to tell me.'

'Tell you?' Philippa said faintly. 'I'm not trying to tell you anything. I—I just thought it suited you. It can be changed if you don't like it—you don't even have to sleep there, there are other rooms——'

'And would you rather I chose one of them? Is that it?' He was very close now, his masculinity almost overpowering. Philippa stared up at him as he came up against her, his rock-like chest crushing her small breasts. 'Look, Philippa, if there's one thing I don't go for it's a woman who blows hot and cold. I just want to know what it's to be, that's all. When we first talked about this marriage you laid down certain conditions— the main one being that it was to be in name only. Not—now, what were your words? Not "free access for a spot of sex", was that it? "No more kisses—or anything." Or did I mishear you?'

Philippa felt her body shudder against him. 'Yes,' she whispered, 'I said that. But——'

'But nothing! All these weeks I've respected that. I haven't touched you in any way. And I suspect that's the way you'd like it to stay—or think you do. Right?'

If only she knew, Philippa thought agonisedly. At this moment she wanted nothing more than for him to take her in his arms, hold her close, kiss her and love her—do what he would with her. But that was only because he *was* close, surely—it was nothing more than sheer animalism, the lust of a man and woman when they were physically close. She was ashamed that she could feel this way—she would be even more ashamed if she gave in to it.

'Yes,' she managed, drawing on all her reserves of willpower. 'Yes, that's the way I want it.'

'Then why in hell's name that sexy bedroom?' he rasped. 'You couldn't have put it more plainly if you'd tried! That room *smells* of sex, Philippa—the colours, the jungle print, the fur—don't try to tell me you didn't *realise*! Do you really mean to tell me you thought that room out, chose the décor and saw it in its finished state without realising that you were making a very explicit statement about us and our relationship?'

'No! No, I swear, I never thought—I never meant—it just seemed to *suit* you, that's all! I thought you'd *like* it!'

'*Like* it?' he said again. 'Oh, my *God*!' With a violent movement he wrenched himself away from her, pressing his hands against the opposite wall and thrusting against them as if he wanted to push the whole house over. 'And just what were you planning to do after that?' he asked in a low tone. 'Say a sweet goodnight and retreat to your own boudoir? Go back to that bedroom you've had since you were a child, with its shelf of *The Wind in the Willows* and *Peter Pan* and its collection of little china animals? Sleep under the flowered duvet, still an innocent virgin, alone?'

There was a long silence. Philippa stared at his unyielding back. She felt dazed and bewildered. She hadn't yet grasped the full implications of what he'd said; she only knew that he was furiously angry.

'Well—yes,' she said at last, her voice uncertain. 'That—that was our arrangement, wasn't it? Zane, I——'

Zane whipped round from the wall. He didn't approach her again; he stood, several feet away, smouldering with an anger that Philippa still couldn't fully understand, and his eyes blazed with scorn as they raked her slim body in the cream lace dress. 'The innocent bride,' he snarled at last. 'You just want it all

ways, don't you, Philippa? I hadn't even begun to
realise just how much you do want—Bethou, marriage,
your independence, your innocence, for what that's
worth, and sex. Oh yes—you needn't make any more
of your maidenly protests. It's sex you want—that
bedroom upstairs spells it out loud and clear. You just
don't want to admit it—you want to pretend to say no,
right up to the last minute.' His tone seared her with its
contempt. 'Well, if you're the kind of girl who only
enjoys being taken by force, Philippa, you can forget
it—I've never had a woman that way yet, and I don't
mean to start now, least of all with my own wife. Like
you said, I can always sleep in another room!'

Philippa heard his words with a kind of incredulous
incomprehension. What on earth was he talking about?
But even as she wondered, she knew that deep down she
had a niggling, uneasy feeling that there might be
something in what he said. It was a feeling she didn't
want to explore. Quickly, driven into a defensive corner
that left her with no alternative but to attack, she hit
back.

'Sex?' she bit at him. 'Is *that* what you think it's all
about? Oh, you couldn't be more wrong! Love, yes—
that's worth having, and when you have that the rest
follows naturally. But sex—no, that's right out, Zane,
with you. Because you'll never love me and I'm quite
certain I'll never love you. You see, I'd never love
anyone I couldn't trust. I'd never love anyone who
could deceive me!'

She felt better for that and stood proudly under his
scrutiny, delighted to see the colour recede from his
face, leaving him pale under the deep tan. 'And don't
pretend you don't know what I mean,' she ended
triumphantly. 'You told me your name was Kendrick—
you never mentioned that that was just your second
name, that your surname is really the same as mine. So
just what were *you* playing at, Zane Kendrick *Ozanne*?
Who are you—why did you come here—and just what
*is* our relationship? Maybe we're not even married at
all. I think I'm entitled to the truth—don't you?'

# CHAPTER FIVE

ZANE looked at her for a long minute, his eyes shuttered. He seemed to be considering his next move, but Philippa wasn't in a mood to await his decision. She'd been through too much strain already that day.

'The truth, Zane,' she demanded imperiously, and saw his eyebrows go up. 'Just who are you—and why was Bethou so important?'

'Let's have that tea, Philippa,' he said, his voice quiet. 'All right, I'll tell you. But we both need that tea, and since you've made it I suggest we conduct this conversation in a civilised way, sitting down with the pot between us.' He stopped her as she moved to put the tray on the kitchen table. 'No—in the sitting-room.'

He took the tray from her and carried it through, setting it down on the low table by the window. Philippa hesitated, then chose an armchair facing the view across the strait. A few holidaymakers were picking their way cautiously across through the rocks; she wondered idly if Hubert had remembered to chalk the times of the tide up on the board that morning.

Zane took the opposite armchair and watched her face. He poured the tea and handed her a cup. His face was serious, but he didn't seem at all embarrassed. Not even by his own deceitfulness, she thought resentfully, and waited with barely concealed impatience for him to begin.

'You saw my name on the register,' he said at last. 'That was stupid of me—I'd forgotten I'd have to sign that with you there. Up to now I'd managed to make any signatures that were needed without you around.'

'So you didn't mean to tell me? You didn't want me to know the truth?' Her voice rose with indignation and he raised a hand.

'I *did* mean to tell you, Philippa. I wanted to choose my own moment, that's all. A moment when you were receptive, in sympathy. Not—as you are now—hostile and angry.'

'And whose fault's that?' she spat at him, and he inclined his head.

'I've already said it was stupid of me. But believe me, I did have my reasons.'

'I don't care what your reasons were. I just want to know the truth—am I married to you or not?'

'And I wonder just which answer you'd prefer,' he mused wryly. 'Well, to put you out of your misery, Philippa—unless it's to plunge you further in—yes, we are married. You are my legal and only wife. Mrs Zane Kendrick Ozanne. And presumably our "arrangement" still stands. What's in a name, after all?'

'A great deal,' Philippa said, her voice tight. 'It all depends on how you got it.'

'I was born into it,' he replied equably. 'My father was Raoul Ozanne, son of Philippe Ozanne. Half-brother to Colin Ozanne—your father. We're related, Philippa. Cousins—or half-cousins, as I suppose you might call it. But we're man and wife for all that. There was no legal barrier to our marriage.'

Philippa's eyes widened as he spoke and became two huge dark pools of dismay in her white face. *Cousins*—even if only half-cousins, as Zane called it! He was Raoul's son—Raoul, who had quarrelled with his father Philippe and left him, hurting him so badly that he'd spent a lifetime in a bitterness that even his second wife and son Colin couldn't assuage. It was Raoul who had been indirectly responsible for her own unhappy childhood—for that bitterness had been passed on to her own father, Colin, and had left him unable to face up to the loss of his wife, unable to give his daughter the love she craved, condemned to a life of despairing loneliness.

And this man—*this man* who lounged in her father's own armchair, who watched her with eyes like gimlets so that he seemed to know every thought in her mind, who was so infuriatingly attractive—this man was Raoul's son. And she had married him.

'You knew——' she breathed, her wide eyes fixed on

his face '—you knew I'd never agree to marry you, if I knew the truth——'

'You *asked* me to marry you,' he pointed out. 'But yes—I did have a strong suspicion that you'd backtrack if you found out. And that would have been a great pity, Philippa, because we would both have lost out on something we badly wanted, just because of a quarrel that took place years ago and is no business of ours. Do you blame me for not wanting it to happen?'

'And Bethou,' she continued as if he hadn't spoken, 'that's why you wanted Bethou so badly. I suppose your father had some twisted idea that it was really his?'

'Not exactly.' His tone was still quiet but there was a note of menace in it now, a subtle warning to her not to go too far. 'After all, he never lived here, did he? If he had, it *would* have been his. But surely even you have to admit that he was disinherited by a rather unpleasant trick. *Something* should have come to him. He had worked with his father for years. Was it really right that he should have had nothing?'

'What do you mean, an unpleasant trick? There was nothing illegal in it. He went away—he left my grandfather alone, and only just after he'd lost his wife. What sort of *trick* was that?'

'I can see you've got hold of a completely twisted version of the story,' he sneered. 'Not surprising, perhaps, but you won't even listen to the real one!'

'You haven't tried to tell me yet—maybe because there's nothing to tell!'

Zane gripped the arms of his chair, then deliberately relaxed. Philippa watched him, half scared but too angry to keep quiet now. She could see a vein throbbing in his neck and she tightened her fingers on her own chair.

'Look, Philippa,' Zane said at last, 'there's no point in us getting heated over this. As I said, it all happened years ago—but surely you know why your grandfather and my father quarrelled? It was, as you say, soon after his first wife—my grandmother—died. Very soon indeed. And it was because he was determined to marry again almost immediately and my father objected.'

Philippa looked away. She wasn't sure she wanted to

hear this now. They were on different sides of the fence, had heard different versions of the same story, and there was nobody left to tell them the truth.

'I've seen pictures of *my* grandmother,' she said. 'She was lovely. She had a kind, understanding face. Nobody could have objected to their father finding happiness with her.'

'Not in normal circumstances, perhaps,' Zane agreed. 'But my father was young and idealistic when it happened. His mother died when he was only twenty-one and he'd idolised her. He was bitter that his father could even think of marrying again only a few months after it happened. And his father was furious—all the more, I suspect, because he had a guilty feeling that his son might be right. He turned the boy out, and in order to disinherit him he did the only thing possible under Guernsey law—he sold the family home, married again quickly and built the house on Bethou. Because Raoul had never lived in that house and because the second wife now took precedence over him, he could never inherit. There was nothing for him but to leave, and he made a thorough job of it and left the island altogether. To him, it was no longer a home.'

'It tears my heart,' Philippa said sarcastically. 'Oddly enough, according to *my* father, Raoul was a grasping, cold-hearted son who begrudged his father any happiness at all, refused to accept the new wife and left them in the lurch just when they needed his help most. It was because he left that my grandfather sold the vineries and went to Bethou, and they lived poorly ever since because there was hardly any living to be made here; just the sheep and the *vraic*—the seaweed—and not much else. There was enough to keep them, that was all, and there was enough money left to keep my father. It didn't take long to go.'

'And you blame Raoul for that? You blame Raoul, in effect, for the fact that your father died penniless and in debt and the fact that you were forced to marry me?'

His meaning was unmistakable and Philippa reacted to it at once. 'Yes, I do!' she flared. 'I blame him for everything—it was with him that all the bitterness began, all the unhappiness this house has seen. Of course I blame him!'

'Then it will probably delight you to know that he wasn't any happier himself,' Zane threw at her. 'He was a Guernseyman through and through, he never really settled on the mainland. He went into the Army when he left the island, almost in the hope of getting killed, I think—that was the last year of the First World War. But he didn't get killed; he went back to England and tried to settle, working on farms and smallholdings, the only work he knew. When he married my mother he took her name, Kendrick, in a further effort to forget, and when I was born he gave me the same name. I still had the surname Ozanne, of course, but we simply never used it. But he couldn't quite forget; he called me Zane as some kind of gesture towards his family—a diminutive of the name he wouldn't bear himself. He still wanted to return, through me if there was no other way. He wanted to make it up—he wanted reconciliation. He tried once—he brought me here, to Bethou—yes, I've been here before. I was a small boy, only about eight or ten years old, but I remembered it vividly all through the years. He wanted his father and his half-brother to see me, in the hope that they would relent and leave the house to me. But their bitterness was complete—it wasn't long after that that your father married, and then you were born.'

Philippa was silent. She remembered Hubert's words, that her father had been disappointed at her being a girl. He had known about Zane, seen him, seen the healthy, sturdy little boy who could inherit Bethou, and he had determined that it would never come about. But he hadn't had a son himself; instead, he had found himself with a daughter, a daughter who reminded him increasingly of the young wife who had died in giving birth.

'You shouldn't have come here,' she said, her voice low. 'You've dragged up all this old pain. . . . Why did you come? Why did you have to have Bethou? Haven't you got enough in your life?'

'If I had, I would certainly not have come,' he said quietly. 'My father wanted me to—he wanted me to have Bethou, he considered it my birthright. I promised him that I would come when Colin died, that I'd keep the house in the family if I could. He had a friend here, an advocate—no, not Henry—who was retained to let him know when Colin died. My father died some time ago, soon after my mother, but the lawyer got in touch with me instead.'

'And that's why you came so quickly. But did it really matter to you? You'd only been here once—it was never your home——'

'I told you, the memory was a vivid one. I carried it with me for thirty years. Bethou, when I was first brought here, seemed to me like Paradise. I knew that when I saw it again it might have changed, or I might. But nothing had altered. To me, Bethou is still the loveliest place on earth.'

Tears stung Philippa's eyes. If only she could have loved this man—if only they could have been in sympathy! Life on Bethou for two people who loved both it and each other could have been, as Zane had put it, paradise. As it was, she suspected that it might be nearer hell. For if ever there had been a barrier to their loving—and oh, there had, there had!—it was an insurmountable one now. Between them lay the rancour of generations, a quarrel that could never be healed. Whatever the truth, nobody would ever know who was most at fault. She and Zane stood on opposite sides and there could be no crossing over.

The tea had gone cold; neither of them had touched it. Philippa shifted in her chair, realising suddenly how stiff she had become. She glanced out of the window; the holidaymakers, gay in their coloured shorts and swimsuits, were making their way back across the causeway. A glance at her watch told her that the tide would be coming in within half an hour and she and Zane would be alone on Bethou to begin the married life that seemed to be even more of a charade than she had expected.

'You'd better take the tractor over,' she said dully,

wishing that Zane would somehow get marooned on the main island and knowing that he wouldn't. 'You haven't got much time. I—I'll make some more tea for when you get back.'

'Yes.' Zane stood up and came over to her, oddly hesitant. He reached out a hand and laid it on her shoulder. 'Philippa——'

Philippa swung round with more force than she would have believed herself capable of. She struck at his hand, sweeping it from her shoulder, and at the same time shot up from her chair, facing him across its bulk. 'Leave me alone, Zane Kendrick Ozanne!' she blazed, her eyes tawny with rage. 'You've told me a very sad story—but I just happen to know another. I happen to know how unhappy *my* father was—so unhappy that he forgot how to love, or how to take the love he was given. *That* was *your* father's doing—and that's something I'll never forgive. All right, so we're married—we've got what we both wanted, Bethou. Let's leave it at that, shall we? I don't want anything more from you, Zane, not one tiny scrap—our arrangement stands just as it was made. And if you don't take that tractor back in the next few minutes you'll be spending your wedding night in Hubert and Margaret's spare room!'

Eyes like chips of splintered steel bored into hers, then Zane turned abruptly and made for the door. He turned as he opened it, and his eyes raked her figure so cuttingly that she felt stripped and moved involuntarily to hide herself from his gaze.

'And for all the wedded bliss I'm going to get here, that's where I might just as well be!' he grated, and then the door slammed behind him with such force that the whole house shook.

Philippa sank down in the chair, feeling sick and weak. She passed a hand over her brow and wondered when this day was ever going to end. It seemed to have been going on for ever—and it was just the first. The first of an interminable procession of days spent here with Zane, each of them irrevocably bound to the other.

What had they done? What had they *done*?

Somehow, over the next few weeks, Philippa found herself settling down with Zane in a kind of uneasy truce. That first day, she had thought it impossible, but she quickly realised that life doesn't deal with impossibilities and that it was within human capability to live with almost any situation. She even had to admit that her own situation could be a lot worse—even if it could also be a lot better.

It helped that Zane was so dynamic. There was no sitting around wondering what to do next—he always knew, and did it. The house was examined thoroughly by experts and decisions made as to what should be done to restore it to the pleasant, comfortable home it should be, and Philippa was faintly surprised to find herself included in these discussions. She would, of course, have been highly resentful if she hadn't been, but she had half expected Zane to take all that completely out of her hands, if only as a gesture. Instead, she was consulted all along the line, and her preferences considered.

Apart from that he had declared himself ready to begin work on a new play. The library became his study and Philippa watched with fascination as he set up his word-processor, showing her how he could store information in its memory and bring them to the screen at the touch of a key. Lists of characters, their backgrounds and idiosyncrasies, flashed before her eyes, and Zane showed her how alterations could be made and his text corrected and made perfect before a word was typed on to paper. When it was all ready, he said, he would print it out on the printer that stood beside the computer, and it would be ready to send away, having taken less than a day to perform what a typist would need weeks to do.'

'High technology comes to Bethou,' Philippa said wryly. 'What a good thing Grandfather had electricity installed!'

Zane flashed her a look at that, but said nothing. He had consistently refused to acknowledge the digs Philippa couldn't help administering, and she invariably finished up feeling ashamed of her incessant urge to needle him. Which just made her resent him all the more. . . . In fact, she was never really sure why she did it—unless it was to gain his attention. . . .

But that was ridiculous! She didn't want Zane's attention. She was happy with the way things were, with him ensconced in his study working, leaving her free to wander on the beaches of the little island or go over to chat with Margaret or even take the car and visit some of the old friends she was now rediscovering. There was always plenty to talk about—the changes that had taken place since her childhood, the marriages and the births—but Philippa invariably found herself steering the conversation away from her own marriage. Yes, wasn't it astonishing, she would agree, smiling, that she and Zane should have come together like this and married. Yes, it was a very satisfying conclusion to the story of Bethou, she would nod, gritting her teeth. Quite romantic. . . .

Perhaps it wasn't surprising that she didn't really enjoy these encounters much and usually found herself driving back to Bethou in a rather more depressed frame of mind than she had set out. Nor very surprising that these visits should become less frequent and finally tail off altogether, and Philippa find herself staying more and more on her island home and rarely going further than Margaret's cottage unless she absolutely had to.

She had grown used to the people who picked their way over to the island between the tides each day; sometimes, when the low tide occurred in the middle of the day and was therefore more convenient for holidaymakers, there were more than at others. When low tides occurred during the early morning and evening few people bothered to come. So she was surprised, one morning, when she and Zane had been married for about six weeks, to see a man walking purposefully over the causeway before nine o'clock.

Intrigued, Philippa went to the window and watched. She wondered if he might be coming to the house. He didn't somehow walk like a holidaymaker—his movements were too positive, there was no lingering to look in rock pools or pick up shells. And besides that, as he drew nearer, she had an increasing feeling that he was familiar to her—that she'd seen him before—knew him quite well even. . . .

And then Philippa's heart jumped and she stared in astonishment. *Could* it be—no, surely not, she'd never let him know where she was—but it certainly *looked* like him—that thatch of fair hair glinting in the sun, the square, stocky build, the way he held his head with chin jutting as if ready to meet trouble a little more than halfway if necessary—yes, it was Kevin. *Kevin*—here on Bethou. Here—presumably, for what other reason could he have—to find her.

But why? She'd made it clear enough, surely— Philippa pulled herself together with a jerk. This was no time to speculate. She must get down there, meet him, prevent him from coming to the house. Thank goodness Zane was already in his study, where his window looked out in a different direction! If she could just head Kevin off—talk to him and find out just why he'd come here—she could probably get him back over the causeway and out of sight before Zane emerged for lunch at midday. After that, she would just have to play it by ear.

It didn't occur to her to wonder why she was so anxious for her ex-boy-friend and her husband not to meet.

Kevin was on the beach by the time Philippa came out of the garden door and he looked up and smiled with relief when he saw her.

'Pippa! So it really is you—I was beginning to wonder, Darling, how marvellous to see you again!'

'Kevin, what on earth are you doing here? How did you know where I was?'

Kevin's light blue eyes regarded her with amusement. 'That's not a very ecstatic welcome, is it? You're supposed to be over the moon with joy, Pippa. This was meant to be a nice surprise for you.'

'Well, it's certainly a surprise,' Philippa answered unthinkingly, and caught the hurt in his face. 'Oh, Kevin, I'm sorry, I didn't mean—it's just been so

unexpected, seeing you appear out of the blue. Look——
—' she glanced back at the house '—we can't talk here.
Let's—let's go for a walk, I'll show you the island——'

'Can't you invite me into the house?' he asked
plaintively. 'I've *had* a walk, Pippa, across that apology
for a causeway. I'd have brought wellington boots if I'd
known what it was going to be like—except that I
haven't got any. Honestly, what a godforsaken spot!
Do you really mean to say this is where you used to
*live*?'

'Yes, and I still do.' Philippa was on edge, in a
ferment of anxiety over Kevin's unexpected appearance
and Zane's reaction if he should come out of the house
now, and she wasn't in any mood to accept criticism of
her beloved Bethou. 'I'm sorry, Kevin, I can't invite
you in at the moment, it—it isn't convenient, we're
having work done and—and—oh, *do* come somewhere
quieter where we can talk. I have to tell you——'

'*Quieter?*' Kevin stared around at the empty beach,
the rocks inhabited only by seabirds. 'You mean there
are places quieter than *this*?' He looked so horrified that
Philippa wanted to laugh, but she stopped herself just in
time; once start and she suspected that hysteria might
set in.

'Do come, Kevin,' she urged, and set off along the
beach, hoping that in the absence of any alternative he
would follow her.

He did, but not very willingly. Philippa glanced back
after a moment to see him stumbling along the rocky
beach, a look of disgusted resignation on his face. He
looked completely out of place in his grey city suit, his
smart shoes probably ruined by sea-water and sand.
Philippa felt momentarily sorry for him, but her own
feelings were too mixed to spare much pity for Kevin's
plight. She wondered again why he had come and what
on earth she was going to do about it.

They rounded the point and Philippa led the way to a
pile of dry rocks on the grass. She often sat here, gazing
across the strait towards Guernsey or out to sea at the
jagged rocks that had claimed so many lives in
shipwreck over the centuries. There was nothing soft

about this seascape, it was hard and cruel—like life, she thought when she was feeling depressed. But at other times, with the sun shedding its limpid morning light on gently rippling waves, or with the craggy reefs black against the blazing flames of sunset, it promised something else; a calm tranquillity shot through with passion.

Kevin looked doubtfully at the rocks but sat down, looking uncomfortable and ill at ease. Philippa watched him, involuntarily comparing him with Zane, who seemed to fit the landscape as if he had been born part of it. She wondered why she didn't feel more excited. This was Kevin, and she loved him—didn't she? But she was still anxious about why he'd come.

'What's happened, Kevin?' she asked at last. 'Why are you here—and how *did* you know where to find me?'

He looked at her and a pang shot through her as she saw the familiar, half-shy expression on the boyish face. He had always known how to enlist her sympathy, she thought irrelevantly, and then chided herself for being cynical. What was the matter with her this morning?

'Vicci told me you were here,' he said simply. 'At least, she knew you were on Guernsey. You sent the class a card, remember? And you said you were living on an even smaller island, so it wasn't too difficult to find out where.'

Philippa sighed and nodded. Of course—that postcard she's sent the children, showing as near as possible where she was. She'd promised them that during her last term, when they'd all been a bit emotional about the parting. Philippa had given her notice in at the beginning of the spring term, knowing that she had to get away from Kevin if his marriage were to have any chance of repair, and it had been fortuitous that before she had time to find another job her father had died, bringing her back to Bethou.

'But why did you come?' she asked again, 'Kevin, I told you, I'm not a home-breaker, I didn't want to——'

'You don't have to be,' he told her quietly. 'Vivien and I have split up again—and this time its for good. I came to tell you, Pippa—and to ask you to come back with me.'

Philippa stared at him. Her mind whirled. Kevin and his wife had broken up for good—and he wanted her to go back to the mainland with him. As his wife? She covered her face with her hands. God, what a mess! What was she going to say? How was she going to tell him?

'Pippa?' said Kevin, and there was a note of anxiety in his voice.

'What—what about Vicci?' she asked at last, more to gain time than because she was really worried about the child. Both parents had loved their daughter, she knew that, and although a broken home wasn't ideal for any child, a great many had to survive it these days, and did. Vicci would be well cared for whatever happened.

'Vivien's taken Vicci with her. It was best really. A child needs its mother and there's no problem about access. Pippa——' his voice sharpened and he reached out to draw her hands away from her face '—Pippa, it's *us* I'm concerned about. You and me. I know why you left—I appreciate the fact that you didn't want to break up our marriage. But you haven't, please believe that. Vivien and I made a mistake and we've decided that to go on together would be an even bigger one. There's no bitterness—and the way's open now for me to be happy. Don't you see that, Pippa? You've nothing to reproach yourself with, you can come back with me the minute you can get yourself organised, and we can be married as soon as the divorce is through. How does that sound?'

His voice was soft and persuasive, just as it had been so many times in the past. It had swayed her then, gentled her into loving him. But now her reactions were different. Something jarred. Kevin wanted her to come back to make *him* happy. He hadn't even asked her whether she wanted to. It didn't seem to occur to him to wonder what might make her happy.

Apart from that, it was all so impossible. He knew nothing of what had happened—and she would have to tell him. And she found herself dreading his reaction.

'Kevin,' she began on a deep breath, 'there's something—you don't realise what—oh, I don't know how to say this, but——'

'You haven't changed your mind about us, have you?' he interrupted, watching her with intent eyes. 'You're not going to tell me that, are you, Pippa? You told me you loved me, you know. You're not going to tell me it wasn't true?'

'No! No, I'm not—it *was* true, I *did* love you, but——' She stopped, aghast. Was she saying that she didn't love him any more? But she did, it was the thought of Kevin that had kept her from giving way to Zane, she *must* still love him. 'Kevin, I can't—I'm in such a muddle.' She stopped again, hopelessly.

Kevin smiled. Clearly, he didn't really believe that she had lost her love for him. He reached out and took her hand, patting it comfortingly. 'Don't worry, Pippa,' he said kindly. 'We'll get it all sorted out. It's been a shock for you, I can see that—perhaps I ought to have let you know. But you know me—I can't resist giving people surprises.' He smiled his boyish smile. 'Anyway, don't you worry about a thing. I'll see to it all. Now, just what's the situation here? I got a rather garbled story from some old boy on the main island. Your father died, is that right?'

'Yes, that's right.' Philippa's voice was faint. She looked at Kevin's hand holding hers and noticed how smooth and white it was. 'He left the island and the house to me.'

'So all this belongs to you?' A speculative look came into Kevin's eyes as he assessed his surroundings. 'Hm. You could do quite well out of this, Pippa. What condition is the house in?'

'We—it's being renovated.' Philippa bit her lip. She was going to have to tell him about Zane—why didn't she get on with it?'

'Well, that's going to be quite a healthy little nest-egg,' Kevin said heartily. 'Could make quite a difference to us—did I tell you old Roberts has been wanting me to go in with him? Anyway, let's have a look at the place—get some idea of what it's worth. A lot of people want to come to Guernsey, you know, as a tax haven.'

'I know.' Philippa felt tired. She just couldn't go all through that again. 'But it's not possible, Kevin. Bethou can only be sold to an islander. Don't ask me to explain, it's too complicated—just believe me. And anyway, I'm not selling.'

It was out. From this point the conversation would follow naturally and she wouldn't have to make a bald statement. Not that that seemed to make it any easier as Kevin, already on his feet, turned and stared down at her, his face a picture of astonishment.

'*Not selling?* But Pippa, why on earth not? You're not planning to *stay* here?'

'I am,' Philippa said bravely. She got to her feet too and faced him. 'Kevin, I'm sorry—I've been trying to find a way to tell you this—but I can't leave Bethou now, it's my home and I'm ma——'

'*Can't leave Bethou?*' Kevin broke in, his face white. 'Pippa, what is this? Have you gone crazy, stuck here on this godforsaken island, is that it? Of course you can leave Bethou! You can sell it, you can——'

'Kevin, I *can't*!' Philippa interrupted desperately. 'I can't sell Bethou because it isn't mine any more——'

'*Isn't yours?*' Kevin's face was livid now, his eyes bulging as he tried to take in what she was saying. 'But you just said it *was*—you said your father had left it to you——'

'He did! And it seemed as if I'd have to sell it—to pay off debts. But since then I've—I've——' she took another deep breath '—I've got married, Kevin, and the house belongs half to me and half to my husband.'

There was a deadly silence. Philippa smoothed a shaking hand over her dark hair and sat down again abruptly. Her legs were trembling and her heart was thundering. Something had happened to her breathing and she took several deep breaths to steady it.

Kevin stared down at her. He was still pale and a nerve throbbed in his temple. His hands were curled almost into fists at his side, and Philippa wondered suddenly just what had gone wrong between him and his wife.

'Did I hear you right then, Pippa?' he said at last in a curiously toneless voice. 'Did you really say that you were married?'

Philippa nodded. Now that it was out at last, she was conscious of a great relief. But she knew that this encounter was far from over.

'Married,' he repeated. 'And you swore you'd always love me. I believed you, Pippa. I really believed you.' He sat down again on the rock, staring out at the sea. 'All this way to find the girl I love, and she's married someone else!'

Tears sprang to Philippa's eyes. 'Oh, don't take it like that, Kevin,' she begged him. 'What did you expect me to do? I thought we'd parted for ever. It was all over— you were going to make it up with Vivien. I never dreamed you'd come to look for me. And when I found out about Bethou—and Zane came along——'

'Zane? Your husband?' There was a curl to his lip as he said the word. 'I must meet this Zane, this paragon. I suppose *he's* never been married, never found himself unable to offer the girl he loves the kind of life she wants. Never found that when at last he could and went to fetch her, she'd forgotten him and married someone else——'

'Kevin, I never forgot you! It wasn't like that at all.' Philippa hesitated; then, feeling vaguely disloyal, she went on: 'Zane and I—it's not an ordinary marriage, Kevin. I told you my father left me Bethou. He also left me a lot of debts. I was going to have to sell it—and then Zane came along and wanted to buy it, but because he wasn't an islander I couldn't sell it to him, so we got married instead. That's all.' Even to her ears the story sounded wildly improbable, and she wasn't surprised when Kevin looked at her sceptically.

'That's *all*? Pippa, it sounds completely mad. You seem to have taken leave of every sense you had since you came here. *Why* couldn't you sell it to him? And why, if *that* wasn't possible—though I can't understand why it shouldn't be—couldn't you sell it to someone else? Why did you have to marry him and tie yourself down here for the rest of your life? It doesn't make sense, Pippa.?'

'But I'm not tied down,' said Philippa. 'I love it here. I don't want to leave Bethou.'

Kevin stood up and took a long, slow look around the island. He looked at the grass and the gorse, at the brambles and the tumbled rocks. He looked at the sands, stretching away towards the main shore, dark with their clutter of seaweed-clothed boulders. He looked at the seabirds that wheeled above, the terns and the gulls and the sandpipers. Finally he looked down at Philippa.

'You want to stay here?' he said, and his tone was incredulous. 'Pippa, you *have* gone mad! There's nothing *here*. Oh, it's fine for a holiday, I grant you that—but to *live*. . . .' His voice trailed away as he shook his head in incomprehension.

Philippa stirred the grass with her toe. She felt uncomfortable; Kevin had come a long way believing that she would be overjoyed to see him, and had been faced with all this. She hadn't even kissed him. He must be feeling totally bemused.

On the other hand, she had never asked him to come. She had genuinely believed that she had seen him for the last time several months ago, that he didn't even know where she was. Hadn't she been right try to make a new life for herself?

And she had to admit that here on Bethou Kevin seemed a different person. Out of his element; out of control. No longer the suave yet boyish admirer who had won her heart in Coventry.

'I'm sorry, Kevin,' she began awkwardly. 'I know all this must have been a shock to you——'

'A *shock*!' Kevin's voice rose shrilly. 'That's an understatement! But I'm not leaving it at that, Pippa, I warn you. I'm not giving up that easily. You belong to me—and I'm going to see that all this mess is cleared up. You're not staying here, Pippa, trapped into a forced marriage. There must be something we can do to sort things out. Don't you worry—I'll see to it. Seems it's a good job I did come without letting you know—or

God knows what this brute would have done to prevent us meeting.'

Philippa scrambled to her feet. 'Kevin, what are you talking about? I'm not trapped in a forced marriage—and there's nothing you can do about it! It's done—Zane and I are married, and that's all there is to it.'

'Is it?' The boyish eyes were hard now and she flinched away from their insinuating look. 'Tell me, Pippa, do you love this man? This—*Zane*? Did you marry him because you loved him? The truth, now—I'm entitled to that, surely!'

Philippa closed her eyes as a vivid picture of Zane's face came into her mind. Strong and lean, with bright sapphire eyes and shaggy dark brows. The thick black hair with its wing of white ... strong teeth that flashed in a devastating smile. ... No hint of boyishness there, she thought. Only the powerful strength of mature masculinity. ...

'*No!*' she gasped, jerking her eyes open. 'No, I don't love him—I told you, it was just to keep Bethou——'

'So you've never slept with him.' It was a statement more than a question, but once more it conjured up visions in Philippa's mind. Zane, holding her in arms that felt like iron bands yet cradled her as comfortably as if she were a baby; fingers that caressed her as gently as if she were spun glass, yet could tighten like steel around her wrist when she tried to escape; a body that was broad and hard, yet lean and muscular. And she thought of that bedroom; the jungle-print bedroom that Zane had said meant sex and that he had never yet used. ...

'I—I can't answer that,' she muttered feebly, and Kevin gave a satisfied grunt.

'You haven't, Pippa. And you know what that means, don't you? Your marriage is no marriage at all—it can be annulled. You don't even have to carry the stigma of divorce.'

Philippa flung up her head and looked him wildly in the eye. 'No! I can't do that, Kevin! Zane and I are married—'

'Not in any real sense.'

'But we are! And that's the way it's got to stay. It's done, Kevin—accept it and go away—leave me alone. This is my life now——'

'But it doesn't have to be,' he argued. 'It's only your life because you thought there was no future for *us*. Now I've come to tell you that there *is*. That alters everything, doesn't it? You can forget Bethou now—forget this man, this adventurer who's conned you into a marriage you never really wanted. You can come back to the mainland with me, and we can start our own life together, just as we planned.'

Philippa didn't remember ever planning a life with Kevin; she'd been too aware of Vivien's existence to do that. But she couldn't argue with Kevin over that point. She shook her head, despairing of ever making him understand. She wasn't even sure she understood herself. So much of what he said made sense. She *had* said she loved him—she *had* wanted to spend her life with him, even if it had seemed impossible. So why wasn't she now throwing herself in his arms, making plans as he wanted her to, preparing to leave Bethou and Zane without a backward glance?

'What is it with this Zane anyway?' Kevin asked, and every time he spoke Zane's name his lip curled in a sneer. 'Why hasn't he wanted to sleep with you? Isn't he normal?'

Normal! If only you knew, Philippa thought, a bubble of hysteria rising in her throat. Then she glanced up and looked over Kevin's shoulder and her blood froze. *Now* what was going to happen? For a split second she wished that she had never got up that morning, or that she could go back now to that moment of waking and find it was tomorrow and all this was over. Then a strange fatalism took over. There was obviously nothing she could do to alter the course of events, so she might just as well step back and let things happen as they would. It might even be easier to pretend that it all had nothing to do with her anyway.

Not that she would be allowed to do that. The look on Zane's face as he strode grimly across the tussocky grass towards them told her that she wouldn't be allowed to opt out for a second.

'Well?' Kevin persisted. 'Is that it? Is he a man, Pippa—or isn't he?'

'You'll be able to see for yourself in about thirty seconds' time,' Philippa said faintly. And then, as Zane reached them and Kevin swung round belligerently, she stifled the giggle of pure nerves that threatened to burst through her lips and said: 'This is Kevin Brant, Zane. And Kevin—this is my husband. Zane Kendrick Ozanne.'

## CHAPTER SIX

THERE was a long silence as the two men stared at each other. Philippa was suddenly aware of the screaming of gulls, the splashing of waves on rock and the bleat of a sheep from somewhere over the hump of the island. Over on the far shore she could see Hubert moving about in front of his cottage and she was thankful that he hadn't come over to Bethou that morning. His presence would have made the situation even more embarrassing.

Zane spoke first. His voice was casual and easy, for all the world as if he were meeting a liked acquaintance, but Philippa could see the cold watchfulness in his eyes.

'Good morning, Mr Brant. You're a friend of Philippa's, I take it? I expect she's been telling you all our news.'

There was a very slight emphasis on the word 'our'. Kevin hesitated, then reluctantly took the hand Zane held out. He gave Philippa a glance she couldn't quite fathom, but it was obvious that he hadn't been prepared for Zane to be the man he was.

'Yes, I'm Kevin Brant,' he answered, and the arrogance in his voice sounded brash and defensive 'Pippa and I knew each other in Coventry.' He was clearly uncertain as to whether to say more and Philippa stepped in quickly.

'Kevin was over here for a holiday and thought he'd

look me up,' she explained brightly. 'Wasn't that kind of him, Zane? I didn't want to disturb you while you were working, so I brought him out here for a chat before lunch.' She turned to Kevin. 'You are staying to lunch, aren't you? One of us can row you back if you have to go before the causeway's clear again.'

The two men looked at her with wildly differing expressions. Kevin was frankly bemused, still bewildered by their argument and even more puzzled by Philippa's treatment of him as a casual acquaintance who had decided to look her up. Zane was blatantly sceptical. But what else could she have done? she asked herself desperately as they made their way back to the house. The idea of telling Zane why Kevin really had come to Bethou was out of the question.

It was still too early for lunch, so Philippa made coffee, wondering rather frantically as she did so just what the two men might be talking about in the garden, where they had elected to sit. She did the job as quickly as possible, carrying the tray out to them and smiling brightly. Please, she prayed, please let Kevin give up this crazy idea. Please let him see how impossible it is. . . . But one look at his face told her that her prayer was unlikely to be answered. His expression was grim, no longer boyish, and with a sinking heart she recognised the stubborn look she had seen on the faces of children who were determined to have their own way regardless of consequences.

'Oh, there you are, darling,' Zane said casually, and her heart jolted at the endearment. He'd never called her that before. And he was only doing it now, she realised ruefully, because of Kevin's presence. Staking his claim. 'I've been telling Kevin,' he went on, 'about our wedding. It was a shame you didn't think to ask him along. He obviously has all your best interests at heart. Why didn't you tell me you had such a good friend back in Coventry?'

Philippa cast him an appealing look. Did he *have* to make things worse? Kevin's face was like thunder now and she felt momentarily sorry for him. It was bad enough for him to come all this way to find her married, without having it thrust down his throat like that. She caught Zane's eyes on her and blushed, then was immediately angry. With herself, for reacting at all—and with Kevin for having put her in this impossible position. Her pity vanished—it was his own fault. He should never have come. Why couldn't he have accepted her departure from his life? Why couldn't he make a success of the marriage he had?

Kevin took the mug of coffee she offered him and set it down rather hard on the grass. He clearly meant to say something and Philippa tried desperately to forestall him with some remarks about Guernsey and the places he ought to visit during his holiday. But he wasn't having any. He lifted his hand and Philippa's voice trailed into silence. She saw Zane watching her with sardonic amusement.

'Look, I'm sorry, but I didn't come all this way to play games,' Kevin said. 'I came to find Pippa. I understood there was something between us—but when I get here I find she's married to you. Can you give me any explanation for this?'

'Certainly.' Zane's drawl was a direct contrast with Kevin's rather pompous indignation. 'Point one—you obviously misunderstood what was between you and Philippa.' He used her full name ironically. 'Point two, she married me because she wanted to. Do I need to go into any more detail?'

Kevin's face whitened. 'Yes, I think you do. Back there on the beach, Pippa told me she didn't love you. She quite positively and definitely told me she didn't love you, she'd married you just to keep Bethou. Now, I don't know if you were aware of this or not——'

'I was,' Zane cut in, his voice clipped. 'And I suggest that it's none of your business, Mr——'

'And that's just what it *is*!' Kevin went on triumphantly. 'Because she *does* love *me*—or did, back in Coventry. OK, she's got herself in a muddle over this house and she didn't think there was any future for us—but now I've come to tell her that there is. She can come back with me and we can get married, and I'm going to see to it that that's just what she does!'

'Oh, you are, are you?' The casual drawl had gone, to be replaced by a metallic harshness that had Philippa cringing. But Kevin didn't seem to notice it as he went on.

'Too right I am! Look,' he dropped his voice to a softer tone, the tone that had swayed Philippa once, it seemed a hundred years ago, 'we're both men of the world, we know how these things can happen. Pippa's just a kid—she lost her father, lost me and didn't know where she was for a while. Easy to see she'd fall into the arms of the first guy who came along, especially when it meant keeping the home she'd grown up in. But that's all it was, we all know that. Now it's all changed. You can get a quiet annulment and no hard feelings. Like I said, these things happen.'

'And Bethou?' Zane's voice was controlled and quiet, but it held a menace that made Philippa shiver.

'Oh, we can come to some arrangement about that, surely? You're in half-possession now, as I understand it. Presumably you'd be allowed to buy out Pippa's share. That way we all get what we want, don't we?'

'Do we?' Zane appeared to consider the idea, then he turned his head. 'Philippa?'

She stared back at him, eyes amber pools of agony.

'Zane—I don't know—I can't say, I——'

'But surely it's easy enough,' he said reasonably. 'You leave me, we get the marriage dissolved, I buy out your share of Bethou and you go back to Coventry with Kevin. Isn't that what you want?'

Philippa looked wildly from one to the other. They were both watching her—Kevin with an arrogant confidence that she would do exactly as he'd suggested, Zane with a cool inscrutability that maddened her. Why couldn't he show *his* feelings? Did he want her to stay—or didn't he? How *could* she decide, with the two of them staring at her like that?

'Don't say you don't know your own mind,' Zane remarked coolly.

Philippa jumped to her feet.

'What *can* I say? You're tearing me to pieces, the pair of you! What are you trying to do? How *can* I say, just

like that—I'd just got settled here—I never expected
to see you again, Kevin, I was trying to build a new
life—and now—now I—oh, I don't know *what* to
think!'

Frantically, she whirled on her toes and made for the
garden door. The two men came to their feet behind
her, but she wrenched the door open and whisked
through it, pulling it shut behind her. To have either of
them follow her now would be the last straw! She stood
panting for a moment, then set off up the island,
making for the furthermost point where she had sat
that afternoon soon after she had first returned to
Bethou. It was the place she had always made for as a
child when she was unhappy, when her father had been
particularly cold towards her. She had always managed
to find some comfort then in the rocks, the birds and
the endlessly surging waves. Was there still solace for
her now? Or had she grown up too much; were her
problems now too complex for such simple comfort?

It was well after lunch-time when Philippa came slowly
down the island to the house. By now, Kevin must
surely have gone; he wouldn't have wanted to stay any
more than Zane would have wanted to keep him. She
wondered what her own welcome was going to be.

It didn't take long to find out. Zane was in the
kitchen, clearing away dishes. He glanced up as
Philippa came in, and his expression was just as
unreadable as it had been before.

'Had a pleasant morning?' he enquired, just as if she
had merely been out shopping. 'I didn't wait lunch for
you, hope you don't mind. I just had some bread and
cheese—there's plenty left if you're hungry.'

Philippa looked at him uncertainly. He went on
clearing away, hung up a teatowel and gave her an
enquiring glance.

'Something you wanted?'

'Oh, don't play with me, Zane,' she burst out. 'What
happened after I left? Where's Kevin?'

'Oh, the boy-friend?' Zane seemed amused. 'He
decided not to stay after all. He went back. Didn't seem

to fancy the idea of being stranded on a desert island—not like me.'

'Did—did he say anything?' She caught his ironic look and added in exasperation, 'Did he say he'd be coming back, or—anything?'

'To collect his belongings?' Zane said thoughtfully. 'Or what he evidently regards as his belongings. No, Philippa, he didn't. I didn't strive to give him the impression that his journey would be worthwhile '

Oh, he was infuriating! Surely he realised what an impossible position she was in—or was he just enjoying it? Philippa gave him an angry glare and received a bland stare in return. With an exclamation of annoyance, she turned on her heel, ready to stalk out of the kitchen, but before she could take a step Zane's hand was on her shoulder, turning her—not too gently—to face him, and now his expression was far from inscrutable.

'Well?' he demanded, his voice hard as iron. 'Was I right, Philippa—or should it be Pippa? *Would* Kevin Brant's journey be worthwhile if he came back? Would you go with him—or would you stay here on Bethou—with me?'

Philippa's eyes met his, wide with alarm, soft topaz stroking tempered steel. She felt a shock travel through her body, setting up a violent trembling over which she had no control. His fingers bit into her shoulder—surely there would be marks there when he let her go. If he let her go. . . .

'Answer me, Philippa,' he grated. 'I want to know just where I stand. *Would* you go with Brant—or are you going to stay here with me? Because you're going to have to say, sooner or later. You're going to have to make the choice.'

'Choice? What choice?' she flung at him, her head thrown proudly back as she met the icy gaze. 'Whatever I do, you're the winner, aren't you? If I stay, everything goes on as it did before—if I go, you still keep Bethou. And that wasn't my plan at all, you know it wasn't——'

'No, it wasn't, was it.' His face was close and to Philippa's fury she felt the same weakness close in on her, his nearness pulsing out that fatal attraction that had her longing to be taken in his arms. '*You* wanted to be the winner—the one who ended up with everything. You don't like to see it happening to someone else, do you? But this is a trap of your own making, Philippa. *You* suggested this marriage——'

'Do you think I don't know that?' she flashed. 'Do you really think I don't remember it every waking moment? Do you really imagine that I don't know just what I've done—tying myself to a marriage without love, binding myself for life to a man who's got just as much natural feeling as a statue, who keeps all his emotion for the cardboard characters he puts into his plays—if that's not a slander on cardboard? Do you really think I would have done all that if I'd had any idea at all that someone who really loved me might be coming within weeks—if I'd known that the whole horrible charade was going to prove completely unnecessary?'

The sapphire blue gaze narrowed as the black brows came down in a scowl of such anger that Philippa shrank under his hand. She watched, hypnotised, as the fine lips drew back to reveal the strong, white teeth that could smile so devastatingly—or snarl so terrifyingly. 'Please,' she whispered, shaking under the iron hand, 'please, Zane, I——'

'I think we've talked enough,' he broke in, drowning her tremulous voice. 'It's time now for a little action, Philippa. I've stuck to those conditions of yours, but this time you've gone too far. I don't take that kind of talk from any woman, and you've been asking for this lesson for weeks!'

With a swift movement he had scooped her into his arms like a child and marched through from the kitchen to the sitting-room, ignoring her struggles. Roughly, he dumped her on the sofa, then turned to draw the curtains with a quick flick of his powerful wrists. 'Just in case the boy-friend comes back,' he said grimly. 'Though I don't see that it's likely, with the tide running—but you never know.' He turned back and Philippa, knowing that there was no escape, lay gazing up at him in the semi-darkness with imploring eyes. 'And now for that lesson.'

'Zane, please, I——'

'You said that before.' His voice was curt. He sat down on the edge of the sofa and pulled her up into his arms. 'Just what was that man to you, Philippa?'

'Kevin? He—he told you, we knew each other in Coventry and——'

'How well? How well did you know each other?'

Philippa dropped her lashes over her eyes. 'Quite well.'

'Very well?'

'Yes, *very* well!' she flashed. 'Very well indeed! Do you want me to make it plainer?'

'No, I don't think I do.' His eyes searched her face. 'So what went wrong? Why did you leave him?'

'He was married. There wasn't any future in it.'

'And there is now? Presumably that's why he's come back.' Philippa didn't answer and he shook her roughly. 'Philippa, I mean to know this.'

'Yes, there is. He thinks so, anyway. He says they've broken up for good and he's getting a divorce, or she is, I don't know which. He—he wants me to go back with him and we'd get married as soon as the divorce came through.'

'I see.' Zane's brilliant eyes were shuttered and dark. 'And you? How do you feel about this?' Another shake. 'I want an answer, Philippa!'

'I don't *know*,' she cried, the tears slipping down her cheeks. 'I'm so confused—I just don't know *what* I want. I wish he'd never come—everything was all right, or as all right as it could ever be, and now—I just don't know anything any more!'

Zane watched her. She bent her head and it touched his shoulder. Unable to hold back any longer, she let herself fall against the strength of his chest, wanting nothing more than to rest there, to weep out all her bewilderment and find some kind of answer. She let her hands creep up his body, resting against his shoulders, clinging to him as if to a rock in a violent storm. Don't push me away, she begged silently. Please, please don't push me away.

And this time her prayer was answered. Zane didn't push her away; instead he gave a strange, half-strangled grunt and gripped her close. His mouth came down to her hair and she heard him muttering half-audible words against the smooth skin of her neck. Turning her head, she met his lips with her own, and then felt the earth whirl as his mouth took hers with a tender passion that sent fire licking through her body and along her limbs. One of his arms enfolded her, keeping her close as the other hand traced a gentle path down the side of her cheek and slipped down her neck to the curve of her breast. She gasped as his fingers found the buttons of her shirt and undid them without fumbling to seek the warm softness inside; then she felt the tightening of her nipple under his sensitive touch and she whimpered and turned in his arms, pressing herself against him, wanting to come closer, wanting an even deeper intimacy.

Zane muttered something and shifted his position, so that Philippa lay back on the sofa. He stayed quite still for a moment, gazing at the pale breasts he had exposed, then he began slowly to undress her. The shirt came off easily, and the wisp of a bra beneath, and Zane spent a long time kissing her and moulding her breasts with his hands. It was as if he wanted to delay the progress of their lovemaking, to savour to the full every moment of this first time. But Philippa, aware only of her increasingly rapid heartbeats, wanted him to go on, to bring her to the climax of this intoxicating sensation. She arched against him, taunting him with her breasts, knowing instinctively what would excite him, moving sensuously and letting her hands move, shyly at first but with increasing confidence, over his own body.

'My God,' he muttered, catching one hand and lifting it to his lips, 'you're a little witch and no mistake! Philippa, my darling . . . tell me this is the first time— tell me you've never been this way with anyone—and especially not that city gent out there with his smart shoes and his smarmy voice—how you could ever have thought you loved him, Philippa, I don't even begin to understand, but it wasn't real. You're staying with me, aren't you—now that you know. . . .'

Philippa stiffened. Was this the lesson he'd meant to teach her? She'd expected violence, roughness, force—something she could use to fan the flames of her hatred. But Zane was too clever for that, she realised. Too subtle. He was using gentleness and tenderness to win her to his side—he was using the attraction he must have known he had for her, to lull her into a position from which she couldn't retract. For once she had allowed him to make love to her, she couldn't possibly apply to have their marriage annulled. Any life of her own, with or without Kevin, would become out of the question. She would be even more irrevocably bound to Zane, his wife in fact as well as name.

With a lithe movement she twisted out of his arms and scrambled over the back of the sofa. Her movement was too sudden and too quick for Zane to do more than make a wild grab as she skipped out of reach, and she was at the door before he could come to his feet.

'A nice try, Zane,' she mocked from the safety of the doorway. 'But you don't seduce me that easily, I'm afraid. Don't forget the old adage—once bitten, twice shy. I shan't let you get that near me again.'

'And what the hell are you raving about now?' he demanded, on his feet and looking bigger than ever in the dim shadows. 'Philippa, what's got into you, for God's sake? We were getting along fine—making some progress at last—and you have to go and wreck it. Why? Or don't you have a reason—is it just that you're too plain scared to let a man near you? Is *that* why you're still a virgin—because you're too frightened to be normal?'

'It's no use insulting me,' Philippa retorted, confident now that she was sure she had his measure. 'No, Zane, I'm not frigid—but as I told you once before, I'm interested in love, not sex—and you may be very good at one, I'm sure you have lots of experience in it—but you're no good at all at the other. And that's what's important—whether it comes with muscles like Tarzan's and a hairy chest, or in a city suit and smart shoes. So just don't try your arts on me any more, Zane Ozanne—I'll make up my own mind, in my own way, without any help from you!'

'And that,' he said, his voice low and menacing, 'is just what you will not do, little Philippa. Because, like it or not, you're my wife, and that's the way you're going to stay. If you choose to look on it as a trap, that's your choice. Like I said before, it's a trap of your own making. And if you try anything so crazy as going for an annulment—well, I warn you, I'll fight you every inch of the way. And I can fight very, very dirty if I choose!'

Philippa stared at him. She could feel the blood racing through her veins, feel the singing in her ears as he came closer. She couldn't let him touch her again—he was so big, so threatening—there was no way she could fight him off if he was determined. With a sob of pure fear, she slammed the door in his face and fled up the stairs. Only when she was securely in her own room, with the door firmly locked, did she feel safe.

But she couldn't stay there for ever, she realised as she went over to the window and looked out at the glittering sea and the shining rocks. She would have to come out some time—and then what?

It was much later when Philippa heard a sound outside and saw Zane, dressed in jeans and a dark blue guernsey, stride down the beach and set off across the causeway. With a sob of relief, she ran to the bedroom door. Now, at last, it was safe to go downstairs and get herself something to eat—she was starving. She had had nothing since breakfast, when she ate little anyway, and it was early evening now. She wondered where Zane was going. The tide would soon be on the turn, but presumably he knew that. He could always use Hubert's boat to get back.

In the kitchen she cut herself some bread and cheese, and wandered back to the sitting-room. It might be a good idea to keep an eye open for Zane's return, so that she could be safely back in her bedroom by the time he reached the house. Obviously, she couldn't spend the rest of her life playing Box and Cox with him, but just at the moment she wasn't at all sure that he wouldn't continue with his determination to make her truly his wife, and that was a risk she wasn't prepared to take.

The telephone rang just as she was swallowing the last crumbs. Philippa sighed and went out to the hall. She didn't really feel like talking to anyone just now, but she supposed she'd better answer it. When she lifted the receiver and put it to her ear, she almost wished she hadn't. The voice was Kevin's.

'Pippa?' he said. 'Pippa, are you all right?'

'Yes, of course I'm all right. Where are you, Kevin?'

'I'm at my hotel.' It was in the next bay, facing out to sea—you could probably even see Bethou from some of the windows, Philippa thought, and wondered if Kevin's room was one of those. 'Pippa, I had to ring. Is—is he around?'

'Zane? No, he's gone over to Guernsey.' She bit her lip, wishing her voice didn't sound so cool, but she simply didn't know what to say. Once again, Kevin had caught her unprepared, and she still hadn't managed to sort out her confused emotions.

'Look, Pippa, I've got to see you.' His tones were urgent. 'I was just too taken aback to cope this morning—I never expected to find you married. We've got to meet. This can be sorted out somehow, I'm sure of it.'

In what way, Philippa wondered, but she only said: 'It's no use, Kevin. It's done and there's no way out. You'd better go back to the mainland and forget about me.'

'*No!* I'm sorry, Pippa, but I'm just not prepared to do that. We were all right together, everything was fine until you got that stupid idea that you were breaking up my marriage. I could have told you it would never work for me and Vivien, but I could see you wouldn't listen. I wish I had now—I thought that when it really was all over I could come and find you and everything would be all right. I never dreamed you'd go off and marry the first man that came along.'

'He wasn't——' Philippa began, and then stopped. In

fact, Zane *had* been just about the first man who had come along—but that wasn't why she'd married him! She sighed. 'It's just too difficult to explain, Kevin, especially over the phone.'

'I know. That's why I want us to meet,' he said eagerly. 'We need to talk it out, Pippa. Look, if he's not there why not make it now? There's no time like the present, and I've a feeling this needs to be sorted out as soon as possible.'

You could be right there, Philippa acknowledged silently, thinking of Zane's plans for her. Aloud, she said quickly: 'You can't come here again, Kevin. Zane will be home soon and I——'

'It's all right, I'm not suggesting it,' he said soothingly. 'No, you come over here, Pippa. I want to see you away from that damned island. You're a different person there. . . . Come and meet me now, Pippa. I'll drive down to the causeway and bring you back here, where we can talk without being interrupted.'

Philippa hesitated. She wasn't at all sure it was a good idea to go to Kevin's hotel. But on the other hand, he might well be right in suggesting neutral ground for their meeting. And she did want to see Kevin again. Perhaps away from here she would be able to come to terms with her feelings and know just what she wanted to do.

'Yes, I'll come,' she said before she could change her mind. 'I'll come straight away.'

'That's terrific,' said Kevin, the relief warm in his voice. 'Everything will be all right, Pippa, I promise you. I'll see you in a few minutes.'

Her skin prickling with nervousness in case Zane should suddenly return, Philippa hurried to find a sweater to pull on over her shirt and jeans, and dragged on a pair of old shoes. She slipped out of the house and down the beach, keeping a wary eye open for Zane. There was no sign of him and she walked rapidly across the causeway, feeling very exposed. If he came back now she wouldn't have a chance. . . . Her heart leapt as she saw a car turn the corner on the headland and come down to the beach; then she sighed with relief. It wasn't Zane's Saab, it was one of the little hire cars. Presumably it was Kevin.

He was out of the car and waiting for her when she came up the beach, still with the uncomfortable feeling that Zane might appear at any moment. Philippa came up to him and he caught her in his arms, giving her a warm kiss. Nervously, she pulled away from him.

'Don't do that, Kevin. We might be seen.'

'So what?' He held her possessively. 'You were mine first, Pippa, and I don't mean to let you go. I don't care if the whole world sees us!'

'Well, I do.' She disengaged herself and looked round. 'Let's get away from here, Kevin. Zane could come back at any moment.'

'I wish he would,' Kevin muttered, but he opened the car door for her and she slipped inside. Kevin walked round the car and got into the driving seat, then gave her an odd glance. 'Well? Where do we go?'

'Where? Well, your hotel, I thought. Wasn't that the idea?'

'Mm. It could be. . . . On the other hand, I don't want you walking out on me because you think you ought to be getting back to your husband.' He invested the last word with contempt. 'Let's go a little farther afield, shall we? How about L'Ancresse?'

Philippa shrugged. It didn't make much difference where they went, she thought. They were only going to talk, after all. She looked at Kevin as he drove and found herself noticing things she hadn't seen before. That slight blurring of his jawline, for instance—was that the effect of Vivien's good cooking or, more likely, too much to drink? She'd never felt very happy about Kevin's drinking, but had told herself that it was understandable in the circumstances, that he would ease off once his problems were solved and they were married. . . . Zane didn't drink a lot, she'd noticed, and when he did it didn't seem to affect him much. . . . She looked at Kevin again. She had always admired the way he held his head high, seeing it as the sign of a dynamic and positive personality. Now it looked more like the stubborn arrogance of a weak man, afraid to let the world see him as he was. Zane's head was held high with an easy assurance, as if it came naturally, not from a need to prove himself. . . .

*Stop it!* she rebuked herself. What was she doing, comparing Kevin with Zane in this way? They were two different men, and the most important difference was that she loved one and not the other. So Zane fitted in here, looked at home and confident with the sea and the rocks of Bethou, while Kevin looked out of place and ill at ease. Did that prove anything? Did it prove that one might be a better husband than the other?

The road took them along Vazon Bay and then Cobo, past the surfing beach of Portinfer Bay and round the deep curve of Grand Havre with its small boats marooned on the shingle and sand, and finally to L'Ancresse common, where Kevin parked the car. There were few people about now; most of the holidaymakers would be back in their hotels or flats having their evening meal. One or two golfers were making the most of the empty course, but apart from them and a man walking his dog along the beach, Philippa and Kevin were alone.

'We're not far from the excavations at Les Fouaillages here,' Philippa remarked. 'I don't suppose you've heard about it. It's believed to be the earliest known stone structure in Western Europe. The very first stone buildings, here on Guernsey,' isn't that exciting? It wasn't found until 1978—there might still be more finds to make. I've been meaning to come out and have a look—there are quite a few monuments around here. A dolmen, a passage grave, a——'

'Yes, and it's all fascinating, I'm sure,' Kevin interrupted. 'But I didn't bring you here to study archaeology, Pippa. We came to talk, remember?'

He turned her to face him and Philippa looked up into his eyes. Pale blue, without the flashing brilliance of sapphire. . . . She shook herself mentally. It just wasn't fair to go on like that—either to Kevin or herself.

'Yes, of course,' she answered. 'But honestly, Kevin,

I don't see that there's much we can talk about. You know the situation, you've met Zane. I—I don't think he's going to let me go that easily.'

'Why shouldn't he?' Kevin demanded. 'You've told me yourself there's no love between you. Oh, I'm not disputing what you say—the man obviously intends to keep a tight hold on everything he possesses, including you. But he can't *force* you to stay with him, can he? This is the twentieth century, Pippa, things like that just don't happen.'

'I know,' she said wretchedly. 'I can't explain, Kevin. I don't really understand it myself, I——'

'Don't you?' Kevin asked bitterly. 'I'm afraid I do. It's the old, old story, Pippa—not to put too fine a point on it, it's plain sexual attraction. Oh, don't try to deny it—you know very well the man's managed to get you fascinated somehow or other. It's like watching a stoat with a rabbit. Believe me, Pippa, if you stay with that man you're doomed. You may say you don't love him, but you haven't a snowball's chance in hell. You'll end up in his bed as sure as God made little chickens!'

Philippa opened her mouth to protest, but the words never came. Wasn't it just what she'd suspected herself? Wasn't it true that whenever Zane came near her she went weak, felt her heart race, longed to have him touch her? Wasn't it true that she'd been within an inch of giving herself to him that very afternoon—only hours after she'd seen Kevin? She looked at the blue eyes again. They were more perceptive than she'd thought.

'How will you feel then?' Kevin whispered, pressing home his advantage. 'I know you, Pippa. It's love or nothing with you, isn't it—or so you used to tell *me*.'

There was a note of jealousy in his voice as he said this, and Philippa realised that he was hurt and offended that she could be affected in this way by another man. Kevin would have had her in his bed within days of their first meeting if she had been willing; and her reluctance to sleep with him hadn't always been accepted with good grace.

Abruptly, she turned away and walked along the

common. It wasn't fair of Kevin to press her like this, she thought. Seeing him had been a shock, it meant a total reassessment of her life, and that couldn't be made in a moment. Seeing him in a different environment, too, had had an effect. She needed time to get her feelings straight, to find out in fact just what she did feel—about him, about Bethou and—she had to admit it—about Zane.

Kevin was close behind her and she felt his hand on her arm.

'Pippa, don't walk away. Let's talk about it. Tell me what it is that's stopping you from coming with me right now. I'm sure we can find an answer.'

Philippa stopped and looked at him. 'Are you, Kevin? I wish I could be as confident. And how could I come with you now? There are things I'm involved with. The house, the island—they were left to *me*. I'm responsible——'

'Not any longer.' His eyes were hard in the failing light. There would be no sunset tonight, she noticed dully, the sky was overcast and threatening. 'You handed those responsibilities over when you married, remember? That was *why* you married, if I got the story right. Zane is responsible for Bethou now——'

'We're joint owners——'

'And that could be changed. I've been asking questions about these laws. He could buy you out now, couldn't he—and then the way would be clear. You could come with me, he could stay here. End of story—and beginning of new life.' He touched her cheek with one finger. 'Isn't that the answer, Pippa? Isn't that the way to make us all happy?'

Philippa stood in his arms, her heart torn. Was he right? Should she do as he suggested—turn her back on Zane and on Bethou and go back to Coventry, to the teeming city life far from the sea, where life was a constant rush and nobody had time to sit on a rock and stare at a sunset?

'Bethou didn't come between us before,' Kevin went on persuasively. 'Why should it now?'

Because I've rediscovered it, she wanted to say. Because I've rediscovered Bethou and my true self—and because I've found something else as well, something more precious than all the rest. . . .

But she didn't say it. Because until that moment she hadn't known it—and she wasn't sure even now what it was that she'd found.

'I don't know, Kevin,' she said helplessly. 'It's all happened too quickly—I can't think.' She put a hand to her forehead, conscious suddenly of an overwhelming wearinesss. 'I'm exhausted—please, will you take me back?'

An odd look crossed Kevin's face. 'Back? Back to Bethou? But Pippa, have you forgotten—you won't be able to get back now. Look at the tide!'

Philippa whipped round and gasped. The tide had turned and was already creeping up the beach, covering the sands where only moments ago a man had been walking his dog. Ripples of water filled the rocks with a collar of lace, foaming higher even as she watched. Panic-stricken, she glanced at her watch and groaned. By the time they got back to the headland, the causeway would be totally covered and the swirling currents would have rendered it impassable.

'Oh, why did you bring me all this way?' she cried, running for the car even though she knew it was useless to hurry. 'If we'd stayed at Vazon or Cobo, I could just have made it—as it is, I'll have to wait till the tide's halfway up before its safe even to row across!'

Kevin followed her slowly and she stopped and wrenched at the door-handle, turning to urge him on. But the look on his face stopped her in her tracks. All at once she realised just why he had brought her here—and realised too that it was pointless to hurry him. Kevin had got what he wanted—or thought he had. And the wave of rage that shook her then was a hundred times as violent as the tide that was surging to its height all around Guernsey at that moment.

'You planned this,' she said slowly. 'You meant it to happen. That's why you wouldn't take me to your hotel, where I wouldn't have forgotten the tide, where I was close enough to walk back if necessary. You wanted me to be stranded with you, late at night. You're determined to wreck my marriage, Kevin, and you don't care how you do it!'

# CHAPTER SEVEN

KEVIN stopped in front of her. There was an odd, gloating smile on his face, and in that moment Philippa hated him. She turned abruptly and began to walk away.

'Pippa!' he called after her. 'Pippa, don't go—we haven't even begun to talk. Come back, sweetheart—there's no hurry now. We've got all the time in the world.'

Philippa ignored him. She kept on walking along the road, back in the direction in which they'd come. Nothing would get her into Kevin's car again, she vowed, nothing! She heard the engine start, listened to the swish of the tyres as they caught up with her. The car stopped beside her, but she kept on walking, looking straight ahead as Kevin wound down the window and spoke pleadingly out of it.

'Pippa, don't go off like that! It's not the end of the world—I'll get you back, I promise. But what else was I to do—I *had* to talk to you—Pippa, listen to me—Pippa!'

Still Philippa kept on walking, and she could now hear the note of exasperation in his voice as he continued to cruise slowly along beside her, pleading and arguing.

'Pippa, don't be so bloody unreasonable! Look, just stop thinking of yourself and your precious island for a moment, will you, and think of *me*—I came a long way to find you and I didn't bargain for this lot! You've got to talk to me, Pippa, and tell me what the score is. I'm not leaving it just like that!'

Philippa didn't pause and she didn't look at him, but as she walked she began to speak, cutting across the petulant voice at her side and forcing it to silence.

'All right,' she said between her teeth, 'I'll tell you the score. The score is, Kevin, that I don't like being

122

taken for a ride—yes, literally in this case. You deliberately took me to L'Ancresse knowing that I wouldn't be able to get back. It would never have worked if I hadn't been upset—I grew up with those tides—but you took the chance and it worked. And that's enough for me. I agreed to come and talk with you because I did think I owed it to you—but now that score's settled and as far as I'm concerned, we're even. You're not the man I took you for, Kevin, and I don't suppose I'm the girl you took me for. So now will you please leave me alone and go back to your nice cosy little hotel and then go back to the mainland where you belong. I love Bethou, and I'm not leaving.'

'Look, Pippa, don't be stupid—get back in the car. O.K., maybe I shouldn't have done that, and I'm sorry—but I was desperate, don't you understand? I'll take you straight back now and we'll talk tomorrow, how about that?'

Philippa stopped dead. She looked at the anxious face peering up at her through the car window and said, slowly and deliberately: 'No, thank you, Kevin. As a matter of fact, I wouldn't cross the road with you now, let alone go with you in a car. You go on—I'm quite happy on my own. Goodnight.'

Kevin stared at her and his face changed in the dim light. He no longer looked boyish and charming; his face was harshly lined, with a touch of spite in the expression. He crashed the car into gear and his mouth twisted as he said: 'My God, Pippa, I don't know what's happened to you, but you've really changed. I said you were mad and I'm beginning to think it's true. This place has got to your mind—or maybe it's *him*. He's got you on a string, Pippa, can't you see it? You're besotted with him—totally infatuated. Well, I just hope that when you finally wake up you won't regret it all too much—but I'm afraid you will. Oh yes—you certainly will!'

The car shot forward into the gathering dusk and disappeared round a corner, its red lights vanishing from sight. Philippa stood quite still for a moment, gazing after it. Then she shrugged, jammed her hands deep into her pockets, and began to walk again.

As far as she remembered, it was a little more than six miles back to the headland opposite Bethou. By the time she reached it the tide should be safe to cross in the boat. What she was going to say to Zane she couldn't even begin to think. She could only hope that he wouldn't have checked her room on his own return and so would never know that she'd been away.

As she plodded along the road in the increasing darkness, the first few drops of rain began to fall.

It was well after midnight when Philippa, wet and shivering, arrived at the headland. It had rained steadily all the way back and she had quickly become soaked. Her jeans clung uncomfortably to her legs and she could feel rain trickling down her neck from her hair. She wanted nothing more than a hot bath and bed. She was past caring if Zane had discovered her absence, past caring about how he would greet her return. All she wanted was to get home.

Shuddering with cold, she went down the beach to where Hubert kept his boat. The water lapped gently on the rocks. It would take her only minutes to row across, and then she would be home. She reached the mooring-post and felt for the painter, her legs weak with relief and fatigue.

But the boat wasn't there. Unbelievingly, she groped around the post. It *must* be there—Hubert always left it ready, just as they kept their own boat ready on Bethou. Then if anyone was stuck on either side, they could simply use the boat, returning it later. The boat must be there, it couldn't——

And then it hit her. Zane had gone across earlier in the evening. Even as she had watched him she had reflected that he wouldn't have much time, might have to borrow Hubert's boat to get back. Obviously, that was just what he had done, and now there were two boats on Bethou and none on this side.

Philippa stood on the beach and felt the tears slide down her cheeks, indistinguishable from the rain. Was *nothing* going to go right for her? She had no option now but to wait here until the tide went down again—unless she knocked up Hubert and Margaret. They would, of course, have taken her in and made a fuss of her, there would have been a hot bath and a warm dry bed for the night—but although she was tempted, she knew she couldn't face their questions, their concern. No, she would have to stick it out.

But she didn't have to stay out here in the rain all night. If Zane was back from wherever he'd been, his car would be in the shed that was used as a garage. It would be locked, of course—but Philippa had known the trick of getting in ever since she was a small girl. Teeth chattering, she unfastened the door and slipped inside. The Saab stood there, solid and comforting, and thankfully she opened the back door.

With a few minutes she had peeled off her soaked clothes, wrapped herself in the blue tartan rug Zane kept in the car, and was curled up on the back seat, feeling the warmth seep slowly back into her bones. She didn't expect to sleep—too much had happened to allow that—but at least she was safe here until it grew light and the tide went down enough for her to creep back over the causeway and into the house With luck, without Zane hearing her.

It was light when Philippa opened her eyes and stared dazedly about her. Wherever was she? And why did she feel so stiff? She moved uneasily and discovered that she was naked and wrapped in a tartan rug—what on earth——?

Then memory crowded back. She remembered the night before—Kevin's phone call, their drive out to L'Ancresse, her furious walk back in the rain. Oh lord! What time was it? Would Zane be awake now? Would he be wondering where she was—and aware that she hadn't been home all night?

Groaning, Philippa sat up and the rug fell away from her breasts. Now get out of *that*, she thought ruefully, and opened the door to find her clothes. They were huddled in a wet, unappetising heap on the floor. There was nothing worse, Philippa thought, than putting on wet clothes, especially jeans. But she had no option. She reached out a hand—and then froze.

Someone was walking up the beach outside. That same someone was stopping at the door of the shed. And as she watched with a kind of fatalistic horror, the door opened, letting in a shaft of weak sunlight, and Zane stood there staring in at her.

'H-hullo, Zane,' Philippa said feebly, half in and half out of the door.

He paused for only seconds, assimilating his shock and moving quickly.

*'Philippa!'* He was by the car, hands on her bare shoulders, lifting her towards him. 'What by all the demons of hell are you doing here?'

Philippa was suddenly, vibrantly aware of her nakedness. She wriggled in his grasp, trying frantically to keep the rug round her. 'Zane, don't! I want to get dressed—let me have my clothes.'

He glanced down, seeing for the first time that she was naked and that her clothes were lying in a sodden pile on the floor of the shed. 'What the—Philippa, just what *is* all this? What have you been up to? *Where have you been?'*

'I've been here,' she returned, some of her courage coming back. 'I've been here all night.'

'And since when?' His tone was disbelieving. 'I came back at midnight or after, myself. You weren't here then. And you couldn't have come over since—both boats are still on Bethou. I had to borrow Hubert's to cross. So just when *did* you come over, Philippa? And what were you doing?'

Philippa closed her eyes. She must have missed him by less than a quarter of an hour. Not that it would have been much better if she had met him—except that she would by now have had that bath and spent the night in her own bed. At least—a thrill of misgiving ran through her—she supposed she would.

'I came over soon after you did,' she told him wearily. 'I met Kevin—he wanted to talk to me. And——'

'And you needn't bother to say any more,' he cut in. 'I get the picture. All right, Philippa—that's it. I've taken just about all I can stand from you. I've stuck by your conditions through all the provocation you cared to hand me, just because I thought that was the best way to play it. Now, as far as I'm concerned, those conditions are cancelled out. From now on, we play it my way!'

Philippa felt terror mount in her body. She watched helplessly as he kicked aside the pile of wet clothes and turned to her. Then she was scooped up into his arms, blanket and all, and held firmly as he stooped to go through the door. She threw a wild glance around her, terrified that they would be seen, but it was still early and no one, not even Hubert, was about yet. Then she found herself dumped in the tractor while Zane swung himself into the driver's seat and started the engine with a roar.

'Zane——' But her voice was lost in the noise of the tractor and she clung on desperately as the vehicle lurched down the beach. There was no question of escape; it was all she could do to hold on to her blanket as well as remain steady on the tractor. Zane drove without looking at her, his gaze fixed firmly on the winding track ahead. When they arrived at the island he jumped down, came round to Philippa's side and dragged her down into his arms before she could begin to think what to do next.

She stayed passive until they were in the house; there was little point in struggling, and she had to go in anyway. But once inside she looked up into the grim face and begged him to put her down.

'I want to have a bath first, Zane,' she said pleadingly. 'Then we'll talk, if you want to. But I'm cold and damp, and I need——'

'I know exactly what you need, and I'm going to see that you get it,' he broke in ruthlessly. 'And who said anything about talking? I hadn't got *talking* in mind, I can assure you.' He carried her up the stairs, ignoring her increasingly frantic efforts to escape, his arms hard and his fingers cruel on her soft flesh. 'As for being cold, Philippa—you'll be warm enough when I've finished, never fear!'

'Zane, *please*! Zane, I beg you——'

'Go on,' he muttered, kicking open a door. 'Go right on begging. You're going to beg a whole lot more before today's out, Philippa.' He threw her down on the bed and she sprawled there in an untidy heap, gazing up at him with terrified amber eyes. 'That's it. That's how I've pictured you.' He was beginning to undo his belt, his eyes fixed on her in a brooding stare. Almost paralysed with fear but aware of a tingling in her spine, Philippa turned her eyes away from his, still hopelessly seeking escape—and saw that they were in the bedroom she had decorated for his wedding-present. The colours of the jungle, brown and gold, surrounded her and she realised just what Zane had meant when he said they spelled sex. She moved on the tawny fur of the bedspread and felt its sinuous softness against her skin. The tingle in her spine spread, aching down her limbs and low into her stomach, and she looked back at Zane and saw him standing there, naked and magnificent, watching her with darkened eyes.

'Yes,' he murmured as he came down to the bed and poised himself over her, one hand at each side of her body, 'we're going to use this bedroom as it was intended to be used, Philippa. As *you* intended it to be used. . . .'

Much, much later, with the sun high in the sky, Philippa stirred from her sleep and stretched her body languorously. She felt sleek and contented, like a cat who has been amply fed with cream. She opened her eyes, looked sleepily around the room, and then turned on her side.

Zane was beside her, his face relaxed in sleep. Philippa leaned up on one elbow and looked down at him as if memorising every line of his face. She looked at the thick black hair, tousled and untidy, the harsh lines that were now softened, the strength that even slumber and contentment couldn't hide. Long dark lashes lay against the tanned cheeks, concealing the brilliant eyes, and she longed for them to open, to show her again the expression that had caught at her heart only a few hours ago, at the climax of their lovemaking.

It was difficult now to recall the fear she had felt when Zane had brought her to this room. It was a fear accompanied by a sense of inevitability, as if she had known from the start that this was bound to happen eventually. She had felt her heart kick in her breast like a panicking racehorse, felt the blood sing through her brain, blotting out all other sound. And then she had felt the soft fur under her body and it had been obscurely comforting, as if reassuring her that nothing frightening was about to happen. She had looked up at Zane and seen him as nature intended him to be, a male animal in his prime, and his eyes had told her there was nothing to fear even while his lips moved in words that might have been either threat or promise. And then he had stretched himself beside her on the bed and their bodies had come together with a shock that was almost electric, as skin met skin and each contour, hard or soft, made immediate and intimate contact.

'Zane,' she whispered, feeling urgently that he had to know the truth, 'Zane, I didn't—I haven't—Kevin and I——'

'Ssh,' he said, his fingers on her lips. 'Let's leave him out of this, Philippa. This is *us*—you and me—and nobody else has a thing to do with it. Forget everything. Just let your mind relax.'

Slowly, she had done so, letting his kisses wash all other thought from her mind. And as she did so, her body relaxed too, moulding to his, fitting curves with hollows, softness with muscle. She opened her mouth to his kisses, letting their lips play together, exploring, seeking; moved her body against his, then held herself away so that his hands could move over her, stroking and caressing. Legs met and entwined, arms held each other close, lips touched, parted and touched again. Their whispers mingled and their movements took on an ancient rhythm that has been known since time began. The world faded from consciousness and there was only Zane and Philippa, Philippa and Zane, lost in a timeless eternity of wonder and delight.

It could have been hours or it could have been a century later when Zane finally raised himself on his elbows and looked down at her with a question in his eyes. Dazed, she nodded, and caught an expression that made her heart leap; and then they were together, their passion surging like the incoming tide, advancing, retreating, advancing, retreating until it exploded in a mutual crash as violent as that of storm waves at sea, leaving them gasping in each other's arms, as spent and breathless as the survivors of a shipwreck, washed up on some strange foreign shore.

Kevin was right, Philippa thought in wonder as she cradled Zane's head on her breast. Zane *had* had her fascinated. She *was* totally besotted with him. But it wasn't mere infatuation—she knew that now, with a quiet certainty that made her heart sing. It was love that she felt for Zane. Love that had kept her here, tied to him more firmly than she had ever been tied to Bethou; love that had kept her from going to Kevin, had confused her when she had tried to tell herself she was still in love with the city businessman.

Poor Kevin. *He* had been the object of her infatuation, not Zane. It had been over as soon as she saw him coming across the causeway, looking so out of place, though she hadn't wanted to admit it. Now he would have to go back and pick up his own life without her. But she—she would stay here, living on Bethou with the man she loved, making it the Paradise they both believed it could be.

Zane moved away from her slightly and she turned and snuggled herself into the curve of his body. Later, they would talk and she would tell him how much she loved him. But just now, sleep was all she wanted.

Zane stirred and opened his eyes. He looked straight at Philippa and she smiled at him. After a moment, he smiled back, then reached for her.

'So you are real,' he muttered into her hair. 'I thought it was just a wonderful dream I'd had. . . . or maybe I'm not awake yet.'

'You're awake,' she assured him, moving against him

to prove it. 'Or if you're not, I having the same dream. Lovely, isn't it?'

He chuckled and slid his hands over her body. 'Witch! I thought you were an innocent! You're a very quick learner, I'll say that for you.' He laid his lips on hers and they clung together, rocking slightly, their legs twining, bodies pressed close. 'My God, Philippa, but you're dynamite,' he muttered hoarsely.

'Must come naturally,' she murmured demurely, and he tugged gently at her hair.

'I said you were a witch. Now—have you any idea of the time? Do you realise we haven't even had breakfast yet?'

Philippa rolled over and looked at the curtains. A dim light filtered through their tawny drapes, but whether it was morning or afternoon she couldn't guess.

'Better make it brunch,' Zane advised, glancing at his watch. 'And make it soon—I'm hungry! In fact——' he moved in closer again '—if I don't get fed quickly, I might have to eat you. . . .'

With a shiver of pretended terror, Philippa shrank away, then slipped out of the bed. Naked, she stretched herself, quite unselfconscious now. Zane knew every part of her and she no longer felt embarrassed by the way his eyes moved over her, assessing no longer but frankly admiring. Better not to expect too much of him, though, she thought, reaching for a blanket to wrap around herself. That admiring look was fast changing to something else, and they really did need to eat. . . . With a lithe movement, she slipped through the door into her own bedroom, the room she had had since she was a child, and stood for a moment on the threshold, dazzled by the sunlight that streamed in. Yes, it really was a childish room still, she thought, glancing round as her eyes grew accustomed to the brightness. Wallpaper with tiny flowers on, pretty curtains and bedspread, pale carpet. And those books that she'd treasured all her life. . . . Nothing wrong with it, nothing at all. It was pretty, fresh and light. But it represented a part of her life that was past now. Her future lay in that other room—a room that was stamped with a more adult personality, the colours of the jungle imprinting her with the dynamic masculinity that called out a response she had never dreamed she was capable of. In this room she had been the innocent virgin, fresh and unawakened; in the other she had become fully a woman with her own strength and power that matched and complemented Zane's, and bound them together in true and complete union.

'What's the matter?' Zane asked quietly from behind her. 'What are you thinking?' But Philippa couldn't tell him, not just yet. Instead, her heart full, she turned and gave him a quick, bright smile, then stepped into her old room and collected her bathrobe. He was right—it was late, too late to wander down to the kitchen in a dressing-gown. Instead, she slipped along to the bathroom and had a quick shower, then returned to get dressed.

'Wish I'd known you were going to do that,' Zane complained when she came back. 'I could have shared it with you. . . . Still, if I had we would probably never have eaten. And Hubert's coming over about lunch-time—he'll be shocked enough as it is if we're only just beginning our breakfast.'

'We'll tell him it's an early lunch.' Philippa evaded his hands and slithered into a clean pair of jeans. 'And it'll be ready in fifteen minutes, Zane, so don't take all day shaving!'

'As if I would!' He caught her and held her to him, passing his hand over her flat stomach. 'What do you think we've done, Philippa?' he murmured against her ear as she sighed and stretched back against him. 'Do you think we've already provided Bethou with an heir?'

'An heir?' Philippa turned her head and looked into his eyes. 'What do you mean?'

'A son. A son to carry on and inherit the island. *Our* son—yours and mine.'

Philippa drew away and looked at him, a tiny frown creasing her smooth brow. 'Would it matter to you if we had—or hadn't? *Does* it matter to you, Zane? Do you want an heir so badly?'

His eyes glimmered. 'Well, it would consolidate my

position, wouldn't it?' he remarked. 'I mean, there'd be no slipping off with Master Kevin then, would there? You'd have to stay if we were to have a son—you wouldn't want to bring him up on the mainland, away from his home, and anyway I wouldn't let you.'

Philippa felt breathless. Was this what it was all about. That lovemaking that had taken her to the stars and back—was it just to make sure of her? Or rather, to make sure of *Bethou*? With a son to inherit from him, Zane's position here would indeed be assured. And if it wasn't—he would have made sure of it for his child. His child—and Raoul's grandchild. Was that, in some twisted way, what he'd been aiming for all along? To get the inheritance back to his side of the family, even though it meant blending with hers too?

'What's the matter, Philippa?' Zane asked, his eyes intent on her face.

Philippa shook her head. She couldn't answer him. She had to get away—to think. Desperately, she looked out of the window and saw Hubert making his way across. He would be wondering about his boat, she thought vaguely, but it didn't matter because the tide was on the turn and he'd need it for getting back. Suddenly she knew that she couldn't face him, couldn't look into those faded eyes with all the secrets that were in hers. She turned and ran from the room.

'Philippa?' Zane's voice came from behind her as she ran down the stairs and she thanked God that he hadn't yet dressed and couldn't follow at once. She twisted open the door and slipped out through the garden, making for the clutter of rocks that had always been her refuge as a child, her 'castle' as she'd called it. She would stay there until Hubert was out of sight, then she'd cross to the main island and lose herself in the maze of narrow roads that criss-crossed Guernsey. Once there, perhaps she could come to terms with all that had happened and sort out the implications.

Sort out her own battered emotions too. She hadn't by any means recovered from those hours of passion that had shown herself a Philippa that she hadn't know existed. A thrill still ran through her whenever she remembered them. But allied with it, displacing the happiness she had felt when she woke in Zane's arms, was a tremor of fear and a deep self-hatred. *Was* that all it was for? Had Zane seduced her simply to ensure that she would stay with him and give him the son he obviously longed for? Didn't he love her as she loved him? Because she had to admit it—she *did* love him. She had fallen in love more deeply and surely than she ever had with Kevin.

With a groan, Philippa turned and pressed her face against the unyielding rock. What a mess it all was—a mess and a muddle. She had lost the man who did love and care for her, and fallen for a man who might have been made of stone for all he really felt. A man whose expert lovemaking could thrill and satisfy her even though it was as empty as a disused well. What kind of a person did that make him—and what kind did it make *her*?

One thing she was determined upon. It would never happen again. She had fallen once, but she would make very sure that it was the only time. And if she was not pregnant now, then Zane would never have the son he wanted. Not from her, anyway.

A cold feeling crept into her heart as she acknowledged that, in that case, neither would she. And her hand moved involuntarily over her stomach as she wondered if it was already too late—if even now there might, somewhere deep inside, be the beginning of a new life . . . a new being, perhaps with black hair and sapphire blue eyes who would grow up and have Bethou for his own when she and Zane were gone. . . .

When Philippa returned that evening she had come to a decision. She had spent all day on Guernsey, wandering roads that had once been familiar to her and now looked strange, different because she was seeing them through different eyes. She had caught one of the island buses and gone to St Martin's, one of her favourite parts, its lush greenness such a contrast from the wild, rocky terrain of Bethou. She had walked out to Icart and stood on the edge of the cliff, gazing along the beautiful, rugged coastline with its golden cloak of gorse; the little harbour of Saints Bay hidden on her left, the larger bay of Moulin Huet safely enclosed by the Jerbourg peninsula. She remembered walking down the leafy water lane, its chuckling stream running down the centre of the paved track, a reminder of old Guernsey.

On her right the cliffs had stretched away, sheer and implacable, to the tiny bays of Petit Bot and Portelet, little coves of white sand and clear water. You could climb down to them from the cliff path that ran from Pleinmont right round to St Peter Port, but because it was so steep not many people did and the bays were nearly always secluded and private. There was always somewhere on Guernsey where you could be at peace, even at the height of the holiday season.

All day Philippa wandered along the cliffs, following their undulations as the path took her around the very edge of Guernsey's south-eastern shores, stopping for coffee at the refreshment room at Fermain Bay, aware that she had had nothing to eat yet unable to face solid food. She went on past Soldier's Bay, where the garrison from Fort George had once bathed. There were new houses there now, the last to be built for the Open Market, an estate for the rich, and she wished that Zane, if he had to live on Guernsey, could have preferred one of these. Then perhaps she would never have met him—*and never known the delight of loving him*, a tiny betraying voice whispered. Nor the agony, she retorted, closing her heart against the longing that swept over her at the thought of his hands on her body, his lips against her mouth.

At last she was almost in St Peter Port, passing the Ladies' and the Gentlemen's Bathing Places—more relics from a bygone age—and looking out at Havelet Bay, and Castle Cornet set halfway along the harbour wall. There were people water-skiing in the bay and she paused to watch them. How carefree they looked! But perhaps they had problems too, waiting for them back on shore. Perhaps they too had fallen in love with the wrong people, or not fallen in love with the right ones.

Bitterly, she wondered if love and marriage ever went right for anyone. In her experience, it seemed unlikely. There were her grandparents—or her grandfather, who had quarrelled with his elder son and sent him out of his life; her own father, so bitter and unhappy after his wife died; Kevin, tossing about in his marriage like a rudderless ship. And now she and Zane. What did you have to do to get it right? she wondered despairingly. What did you have to have?

And then she could put off the moment of returning no longer. She wandered the narrow streets of the town, staring unseeingly into shop windows and knowing that she would have to go back. And that being the case, the sooner the better. The situation couldn't be allowed to go on as it was. She and Zane had to talk, to be absolutely honest with each other, to find out if anything could be salvaged from the mess they had made so far. And if not—well, that would have to be discussed too. Somehow—and she didn't know how—their arrangement would have to be rearranged.

The sky was just beginning to change colour as Philippa arrived back at the causeway, the sun deepening to a flush of apricot, the wispy clouds tinged with pink. Sunset off Bethou, particularly at low tide when the rocks stood out like jagged teeth, was invariably spectacular; Philippa had never seen a sunset anywhere to equal it. It was even better seen from here, she mused as she looked at her home across the wet sand, looking in silhouette like a huge and craggy castle, half ruined but still exerting a power of days gone by. Her castle, she had once thought it, and herself queen. Well, in a way she still was, but she had been usurped from ultimate power. Zane was definitely king now, and she wondered just how and why she had let it happen. Hadn't she known right from the start that he was dangerous?

If their relationship had been in truth what it had seemed to be that morning, before he had made that remark about an 'heir', she would have been happy to call him king of her castle. But now—everything seemed out of key and she just wasn't sure.

Slowly, she picked her way across the causeway. She wondered if Zane had already seen her, what sort of welcome she would get, and shivered a little. Would he be angry—or would he be glad to see her? Whatever his reaction, she must keep her head. Not let him take over, certainly not let his physical attractions—and she shivered again—overwhelm her. They had to talk, and she had to make sure that they did before they went a step further.

She unlatched the garden door and went inside, half expecting to see Zane there, waiting for her on the seat where they had so often drunk coffee together. But he wasn't—and Philippa, with a shock that had her wondering wildly if somehow she'd stumbled into the wrong house, or maybe even the wrong time, stopped with a little cry of astonishment.

The woman who was occupying the garden seat looked up from under heavy, shadowed lids. She was stretched out with languorous grace, an evening dress of shimmering gold falling from a body that was perhaps one of the most voluptuous that Philippa had ever seen. A cloud of pale blonde hair fell shining past her smooth bare shoulders, and her narrow feet, tipped with gold nail varnish, were bare. A pair of flimsy sandals lay on the grass where she had kicked them off.

She glanced up and her eyes moved slowly over Philippa, who immediately felt scruffy and unkempt in her shirt and jeans that, though they might have been clean a few hours ago, now felt hot and dusty. She pushed back her short cap of hair, lifting it away from her forehead, and sought frantically for something to say.

The other woman, however, had no such problems. Without getting up, she held out a slenderly curved arm and smiled a slow smile that didn't reach her eyes.

'You must be Philippa,' she drawled in a low, husky voice. 'Zane and I wondered when you'd be coming back. My name's Nadia—Nadia George. Zane and I are old friends.' There was just the tiniest hesitation before she said 'friends'. 'It's so nice to meet you, Philippa. I've been wondering just what kind of girl it

could be that Zane would marry.' Again, a minute
emphasis on that last word. And the implication, left
hanging in the air between them, that Nadia still didn't
know. 'I'm staying here for a few days,' Nadia added
casually. 'Hope it's all right with you.'

All right with me? Philippa thought as she took the
hand and held it for the shortest time possible. No, it
damned well isn't all right—but she knew that there was
nothing she could do about it. Zane had obviously
invited this woman here, and if he intended her to stay,
then stay she would.

And just where does that leave me? Philippa
wondered as she mumbled some excuse about getting
tidied up and made for the house. There would
obviously be no more talking between her and Zane
now. Again, the situation had taken a turn that left her
breathless and bewildered. Just what was this—*Nadia*—
doing here? And what was she to Zane?

What she had been in the past was easy to deduce.
But what was she going to be in the future?

## CHAPTER EIGHT

BECAUSE they had been alone on Bethou, Philippa had
continued with her father's old arrangement of having
Margaret come over several days a week to clean the
house and cook a meal. In fact, she was doing less of
the cooking, since Philippa, so often at a loose end
while Zane was working, had decided to learn to cook
more ambitious dishes than she had ventured to try in
her bedsitter in Coventry. Their mornings had often
been spent in the kitchen with Margaret overseeing
some of Philippa's attempts at producing the local
dishes. Margaret was a Guernsey cook of the old school
and thought nothing of stewing lobsters, making conger
soup or even preparing ormers—the large, limpet-like
shellfish which needed to be scrubbed, then beaten
tender for half the morning before being boiled for

about six hours, only then being fit to eat. It struck Philippa that the first person to eat ormers must have been very hungry and very determined indeed!

As she went indoors her mind ran over the contents of the kitchen. Margaret hadn't been over for two days, having been to help her daughter with a new baby, so Philippa was on her own as far as producing a meal this evening was concerned. There was a *gache* in the cake tin, but that was hardly suitable for a dessert, although she supposed it would do at a pinch. There was a fresh chicken, she could roast that, and there was a cheesecake mix and a tin of orange segments; she would have to make something with those. Not exactly Cordon Bleu, but it would have to do. Not that she really cared whether Nadia enjoyed her meal—it was simply a matter of pride. Anyway, it was Zane's fault—he'd never mentioned the invitation, so he couldn't expect anything else.

Philippa stopped dead halfway up the stairs. Why *hadn't* he mentioned Nadia's visit? It would have been common courtesy, if nothing else, surely. If inviting his ex-mistress—for Philippa was sure that this was what Nadia was—was reasonable behaviour anyway. And the more she thought about it, the more convinced she was that it wasn't!

All right, so Kevin had come to see her. But he hadn't been expected and he hadn't known she was married. Could the same be said of this Nadia? It seemed like stretching coincidence too far. And how had she known where Zane was? No, he must have been in contact with her and therefore he must have invited her.

A slow anger began to burn in Philippa's heart. That showed just how much this morning's encounter had meant to him! He must, surely, have known even then that Nadia was on her way. Was it a deliberate attempt to humiliate the girl he had married?

Without further thought Philippa swung round and went downstairs again. Zane was in his study working and she thrust open the door and marched in. He was sitting at the word-processor, concentrating on the page of text shown on the screen and making rapid alterations to it, and as Philippa stormed in he swung round, his face dark and angry.

'I've told you never to disturb me when I'm working——'

'And I never have,' she flashed. 'Don't worry, Zane, I won't keep you long. I just want to know who that woman is—that *friend* of yours who says she's going to stay here!'

'Didn't she tell you her name?' he demanded. 'Maybe you didn't ask her. The perfect hostess! She's Nadia George——'

'I know her name! I didn't mean——'

'Nadia George the actress,' he continued, raising his voice above hers. 'You must have seen her on TV.'

'I never watch TV—well, only occasionally. I didn't have my own set in Coventry and only saw a few programmes on friends' sets.' One of which had been *Barnaby*, Zane's serial, but she bit her lip and didn't mention that. Nadia George certainly hadn't been in that, anyway. She was much too glamorous for the underprivileged world that play had depicted.

'Well, be that as it may, that's who she is. She's been in two of my plays and we've been friends for a long time. I invited her to stay—I was going to mention it, but recent—events—put it out of my mind.' He turned back to the screen. 'And now, if you don't mind, I'd like to get on——'

'Well, I'm sorry, but I do mind! Just who do you think you are, Zane, inviting people to my home without a word——'

'I understood it was my home too,' he cut in, his voice cold and hard.

'—and then leaving them for *me* to entertain while you get on with your stupid work——'

'It was my stupid work that helped you to keep Bethou——'

'And not even *telling* me so that I could get things ready! Where is she to sleep, what am I to feed her on, what——'

'Stop flapping, Philippa,' he ordered curtly. 'It's all

arranged. We're eating out tonight, I've already booked a table at the O.G.H. so you'd better go and get ready. As for sleeping, Nadia can have my room——'

'*Your* room?' Philippa could scarcely believe her ears. Surely he couldn't be so blatant as that—he couldn't mean—She felt the colour drain from her face as she took a step forward. No—she wouldn't put up with it, she couldn't be expected——

Zane sighed and looked thoroughly exasperated. 'Stop acting like a fool, Philippa,' he ordered. 'I said, Nadia can have my room. Perhaps I should have said, my *old* room.' He stood up then and reached out, drawing her to him with less gentleness than Philippa would have liked. 'After all, we've christened the jungle room now, haven't we?' he murmured insinuatingly. 'Did you really think I'd move back across the passage after this morning?'

Philippa stared up at him, her heart hammering. Did *he* really think that nothing had changed? Did he think she'd run off in a tantrum and had now come back with her tail between her legs, ready to be forgiven, petted and made love to again? Didn't he realise that they had things to talk about, that their relationship had to be crystal-clear before they took another step?

Apparently he didn't. More than that, he expected her to accept this invasion of their privacy by someone she was sure must be his ex-mistress (only she wasn't absolutely sure about that ex) and behave as if their marriage were completely normal. When they both knew—and Nadia would very quickly see—that it wasn't.

'Oh no!' she breathed, her eyes darkening to mahogany as she looked up at him, tilting her head back in a way that gave her a measure of temporary confidence. 'Oh no, Zane. If you thought we were going to pick up just where we left off, you thought wrong. Move into the—the other bedroom if you like; but don't expect me to join you there. You've had your chance to get yourself an "heir" as you call it—and it's your only chance. If you didn't succeed, that's your own very hard luck!'

Zane's eyes narrowed in disbelief. 'What the hell are you talking about?' he demanded harshly. 'And just why did you go rushing off like that? To see the boyfriend? Some time, Philippa, you and I are going to have to have a good talk about all this—but now isn't the time. It's getting late——' he glanced at his watch '—and if you're coming out to dinner you'd better do something about your appearance. Just at the moment, you look like something the cat brought in! Go and get changed. We'll sort.this out later on.'

'You're darned right we will,' said Philippa between her teeth. 'That's just what I came back to do—I didn't expect to find a *femme fatale* lounging in my garden. And thank you for the compliment, but if you don't mind I won't join you for dinner. I'm sure you and your lady-friend would much rather be alone!'

Zane's eyes bored into hers and she turned away, unable to withstand that diamond-hard gaze. Suddenly she felt very tired and wished he would go. She put a hand to her forehead.

'All right,' Zane said suddenly. 'If that's the way you want it. I'll take Nadia out alone. But remember, Philippa, it was your suggestion.'

'Oh, do what you like,' she said wearily. 'I just don't care any more.'

She looked up as she turned away and caught Zane's glance on her. He looked momentarily baffled, at a loss—but the second their eyes met his expression closed and she saw the guarded, shuttered look she'd grown familiar with.

'I'll see you tomorrow, then,' Zane said stiffly. 'That's unless you choose to sleep in *our* bedroom.'

'I won't do that,' Philippa returned scornfully. 'Enough's enough for any girl, Zane—and enough is what I've had.' It wasn't true, but how could she tell him that, when she was sure it was all a trick anyway? Her own yearnings were the greatest betrayal of all— and she wasn't going to give way to them a second time. Not even to spite Nadia George!

'Hadn't you better go down to your guest, Zane?' she asked scathingly. 'She must be wondering just what's going on—and we wouldn't like her to get the wrong idea, now would we?'

Her head still high, she marched from the study and ran up the stairs to her room; but once there, with the door securely locked behind her, she flung herself down on the bed and gave way to all the feeling that was pent-up inside her. The tears flowed freely, soaking the pillow and streaking her face, though just what she was crying for she wasn't absolutely sure. Was it for a love she had lost, or a love she had never really had? She only knew that somewhere among her shattered dreams there was a picture of a baby—a dark-haired baby with a brilliant eyes and a dazzling, if toothless, smile. A baby that, unless a miracle had already happened, she would never, now, hold in her arms.

Zane didn't come near Philippa again that evening. She didn't know how long she'd been crying before she heard them go out and she lifted her tear-stained face from the pillow and looked out of the window to see Zane leading the actress across the causeway. She didn't appear to like it much; she was picking her way daintily, her long, floaty skirt held up out of the way of the salt water and, unhappy though she was, Philippa couldn't help a small smile at the sight of green wellingtons under the shimmering gold fabric. But it was a very small smile, and it soon faded. Nadia George might look faintly ridiculous crossing a damp causeway in evening dress, but she would look little short of stunning anywhere else. You didn't have to be on her side to admit that.

Sighing, Philippa went down to the kitchen to find herself something to eat. Meals had been on the irregular side lately, she thought ruefully, and she could have done with one of the O.G.H.'s substantial and delicious five-course meals. It already seemed a lifetime since her last visit to the hotel—on her wedding-day.

She took some cheese and biscuits and went out into the garden to eat them. The sun had almost disappeared from view by now, its tip lying on the horizon like a shred of orange rind, surrounded by the dying embers of a summer bonfire. Lights were beginning to appear on the main island, winking through the dusky twilight like fireflies, and a sense of peace lay over the scene.

Except in my heart, Philippa thought, and wondered if she would ever know peace again. She wished she had never discovered her true feelings for Zane. It had been so much easier when she'd hated him!

Tentatively, she let her mind explore the memory of Zane's lovemaking—was it only that morning, no more than twelve hours or so ago? She shivered as she felt again the touch of his sensitive fingers, the way they woke in her a response that was almost savage. She had never known such sensations before—the desire she had felt for Kevin had been no more than a pale imitation. A yearning to have Zane touch her again swept over her, rocking her with its intensity, and she wondered just what his reaction would be if he came home to find her in the jungle-print room. But she couldn't do that— not after his revelation that he simply wanted an heir, and certainly not with Nadia in the house. Suppose he actually brought the other woman to the room—no, it wasn't to be thought of.

Philippa yawned suddenly, conscious of a tremendous weariness. It wasn't surprising—she'd hardly slept well last night and today had been exhausting both emotionally and physically. And she'd be happier if she was safely in bed by the time Zane and Nadia returned. That way, she wouldn't have to face either of them again, nor would she have to know just what happened after they did return. . . .

Picking up her plate and the mug she had drunk her coffee from, Philippa went back into the house. She paused for a moment to look around as she went slowly up the stairs. So much had happened since that first day, when she had returned to find her home unwelcoming and unlived-in. It looked very different now—the floor was polished to a rich sheen, flowers glowed on the small table in the hall, the living-room was comfortably cluttered. But there still wasn't love here. And that was what Bethou needed to bring it to life. It was what any home needed.

In spite of her tiredness, Philippa didn't sleep much that night. She lay watching the sky grow darker, saw the first stars prick the deep blue and watched the reflected flashing of the lighthouse. It was late when she heard Zane's car finally arrive on the opposite shore, followed a little later by the splash of oars as he rowed Nadia back to Bethou.

She turned over then and covered her ears with the bedclothes. If there was one thing she didn't want to know it was just what Zane and Nadia did when they came into the house. Or where they went.

The next few days passed slowly. Philippa felt more and more at a loss, faced with the alliance between Zane and Nadia. Her position as owner of the house had been diluted by what she now saw as Zane's takeover—it was *his* house now, he was making that quite clear, and Nadia obviously believed it. Her eyes were cool and scornful when she looked at Philippa, and seemed to imply that Philippa was simply hanging on for what she could get, and pretty hopelessly at that.

'Fancy you and Zane being married!' she remarked one day, in a tone that said quite clearly that she didn't fancy it at all. 'We were all amazed when we heard. I mean, *Zane* to settle for the pipe and slippers. . . . Not that he actually seems to have done that.'

'Do you mean you never thought of him as the marrying sort?' Philippa enquired, and saw Nadia's eyes narrow.

'I wouldn't have said that,' she drawled in that husky, too-attractive voice. 'Just that—well, let's be frank, shall we? You're not exactly what I saw as his choice, that's all. Well, I've known Zane a long time and I expected someone more——' She shrugged pretty shoulders, beautifully revealed by her brief suntop, and smiled charmingly.

'Sophisticated?' Philippa suggested. She had decided at the outset that it was no use her trying to compete with Nadia's sultry beauty and expensive clothes, and had gone on defiantly wearing T-shirts, shorts and jeans, her accustomed wear on Bethou. She was quite well aware of the older girl's disparaging glances but determinedly disregarded them. What Zane thought, she had no idea; his gaze when it rested on Nadia was admiring, but when he turned his eyes to her they were blank and shuttered.

'Well, if you like to put it that way.' Nadia smiled again, showing her perfect teeth. She must have a wonderful dentist, Philippa thought cattily, knowing that thought was as far as she would get. When it came to being catty, Nadia would win paws down.

'How long are you planning to stay?' she asked, as if it hardly mattered. 'I'll need to do some shopping tomorrow and it would be nice to have an idea.'

Nadia stretched her lissome body, lifting her face sensuously to the sun. 'Oh, I don't really know. A few days—maybe longer. Depends on Zane really, doesn't it?' Her smile this time was brilliant. 'And talking of Zane—I think I'll just wander in and say hullo to him. Haven't seen him yet this morning.'

'He's working——' Philippa began, but Nadia only smiled again and swayed into the house. Oh well, let her find out for herself what Zane's like when he's interrupted, Philippa thought, and waited for the explosion. But it never came; and when she went indoors herself a few minutes later she heard sounds coming from the study. A deep, masculine chuckle; and a husky trill of very feminine laughter. . . .

It wasn't long before Nadia was spending almost all her time in the study with Zane. Philippa, mooning listlessly about the house, unable to settle to any of her usual pursuits, couldn't help hearing them. They seemed to have a lot to talk about, she thought moodily as she passed the study yet again and heard their voices murmuring together. And there was a quality in those murmurs that sent a prickle of unease down her spine. Wasn't that the way Zane had murmured to her when he was making love . . . wasn't it just that note she'd thrilled to in his voice as he'd held her close and taken her to the stars and back? She stood by the door, torn by indecision, longing to burst open the door and afraid of what she might see. . . . Yes, it had been much, *much* easier when she'd hated him! This way, it was just pure agony.

'But what about your wife?' she heard Nadia say just as she was about to turn away.

'Her? Doesn't suspect a thing,' Zane's tones came, easily confident. 'Darling, come closer. You've always known it had to be us, haven't you? Don't worry about her—that was all a mistake. It can be sorted out. . . .'

Her blood cold, Philippa somehow got herself away from the study door and up the stairs to her bedroom, where she leaned shakily against the door. Great shudders shook her body and she felt sick. There was a roaring in her ears and all the world seemed to have fallen away, leaving her swinging wildly in a vast, unprotected space. . . .

Realising that she was about to faint, she stumbled to the bed and fell across it, her head dropping over the side. The roaring eased a little and after a while she felt better. But the sickness was still there, a sickness that came from knowing for certain now that Zane didn't love her, never had, that Nadia was still his mistress. And perhaps hoped to be more—she remembered those words: 'It can be sorted out'—the very words that Zane had used to her only a day or two ago. She knew now just what he had meant.

It took Philippa a long time to face up to the fact that Zane had married her with the intention of wresting Bethou from her entirely—not of sharing it, as she had intended, but of finding some way to make her leave the island, leaving him in sole possession. Only in that way would he have avenged the imagined wrong done to his father.

And only by giving him a child would Philippa have had any chance of keeping her home. Although, she thought with a shiver, there was no guarantee even of that. Zane Kendrick Ozanne was quite capable of waiting until his heir was born before turning her away. At least she had escaped that.

Well, he wasn't going to succeed, she thought with a sudden rush of determination. Bethou was *her* island, *her* home. And she wasn't going to let him hound her from it, she just wasn't! All right, so he'd brought his mistress here, either because he just didn't care what Philippa felt or in the hope that she would leave. Two could play at that game! There was a chance that Kevin was still in Guernsey, waiting a few days before approaching her again. Why shouldn't she invite *him* here too? All right, it was bound to cause trouble—but at least she wouldn't be made to feel an outsider in her own home. At least she would have asserted herself!

Without giving herself time to think, Philippa ran down the stairs and lifted the phone, dialling the number of Kevin's hotel. To her delight, she was put straight through to his room and she launched straight into her speech, ignoring all his bewildered attempts at interruption.

'Kevin? It's Pippa. How are you? I was afraid you might have gone home. I just wanted to say—about the other night—I'm sorry I flew off the handle. I should have been more reasonable.' She injected some Nadia-like charm into her voice. 'Look, I've been thinking— why don't you come over and spend a few days on Bethou? It seems silly, you being over there and me here when we've got so much to talk about. And the silly old tide, cutting us off at the wrong moment. . . . Come over and stay. There's lots of room.'

Kevin got a word in at last. 'Stay? But what about——'

'Zane? Oh, he won't mind a bit. In fact, he's got a friend staying here too, so we'll have lots of time to ourselves. Do come, Kevin,' she added coaxingly.

'Well, if you're sure it's all right.' He sounded doubtful. 'I must admit I didn't like the idea of going without seeing you again—having one last try.'

'You come on, then,' she urged him. 'We'll have all the time in the world. Come over tomorrow—as early as you like.'

Smiling, she replaced the receiver. Zane would be in for a shock when Kevin turned up again, and he wouldn't be able to do a thing about it. Not a thi——

'That was the boy-friend, I take it.'

Philippa spun round, her heart in her throat. Zane

was leaning against the open study door, watching her grimly. There was no sign of Nadia, but that didn't mean she wasn't within earshot. Philippa swallowed and tried to speak without her voice trembling.

'Yes, it was. I've invited him over for the rest of his holiday. I suppose you've no objection?'

'And just what makes you suppose that?'

'Well, you've got Nadia here and——'

'And you thought you'd have someone too. What is it, Philippa? Revenge—tit for tat? Or would you be trying to make me jealous?' He came a step nearer and Philippa backed away.

'Jealous?' she squeaked. 'Why should I want to make you jealous? Why should I care *what* you feel?'

'Why indeed?' His hand came up to her face and the fingertips brushed against her cheek, a mere whisper of a touch but nevertheless it sent a flame licking through her body. 'I ask myself that, Philippa. In fact I ask myself a lot of things—like whether you do in fact care anything about me. And why you behave as you do— like a spoilt child who's had her sweeties snatched. Like a female Peter Pan who's never learned to grow up——'

'I *am* grown up!' she snapped. 'I'm a woman!' And her cheeks warmed as she thought of his lovemaking the other morning. Had he thought her a child then?

'Yes, I must admit I thought you were a woman,' he agreed, reading her mind. 'But not all the time, Philippa. Since then you've been a wilful ten-year-old, and charming though ten-year-olds can be, I'm getting just a little tired of the act. So why not forget it? Be a woman all the time—and stop these silly scenes and this I'll-go-out-in-the-garden-and-eat-worms attitude. Because *I* won't be sorry, you know. The only person who'll be sorry is you.'

'I don't know what you're talking about,' she muttered.

'You do, you know. This invitation to Kevin. You don't really want him here. He'll just cause more complications, and you need them like you need a pet elephant. Give yourself a break, Philippa and admit what it is you really want.'

'And that is?' she demanded stonily, and watched his brilliant eyes glitter with mockery.

'Don't tell me you don't know, Philippa,' he murmured, and bent his head. His lips met hers, parting them easily, and his arms came round her to support her trembling body. She felt his lips play with hers, then move slowly, sensuously, across her cheek to nip at her ear, before tracing a path of tiny kisses down her neck to the opening of her shirt. One hand cupped her breast, moving rhythmically to stimulate her response, and she knew that if she didn't move fast she would be lost. She twisted violently in his arms, wrenching herself away and stumbling up several stairs before pausing to look down at him.

'Don't you dare touch me, Zane Kendrick!' she hissed. 'Don't you dare come near me again. I'm warning you—I won't let you, and I don't care what I do to stop you. How can you even begin to think I want you, when I know what you're doing with Nadia in that study—you disgust me, Zane, you really do. Eat worms! I'd rather *live* with them than with you—but you needn't think that means I'm going to leave,' she added quickly, seeing a flicker in his eyes. 'No, I shall never leave Bethou. This is *my* home—*mine*—and you've no right to it at all. You tricked me into sharing it with you—and all because of some stupid family feud, all because you wanted it back on your side of the family. Well, you may think you've got what you want, but if you want *her* as well I'm afraid you're going to be disappointed. And I don't intend to put up with your *ménage à trois*, either—let's make it a foursome, and then we'll all be happy!'

Zane stared up at her, his face shadowed in the dim light of the hall. She could see only the glimmer of his eyes and the flash of his teeth as he spoke. And the sound of his voice made her quake with fear. It was deeper, colder and harsher than she had ever heard it before, and she knew that if Zane had ever felt any love at all for her, it had all vanished now.

'Happy?' he said, the words dropping like stones into the icy pool of misery that stretched between them.

'Happy? *You* won't be happy, Philippa. And I'm beginning to revise my earlier opinion—I don't think you're jealous either. You're just plain, raving mad. You must be.' He half-turned away, then glanced back. 'All right, have your boy-friend over here. But don't say I didn't warn you. And don't come running to me to pick up the pieces when it all goes wrong. Up to today, I would have done. Not any more.'

He went back into the study and Philippa stared after him, a great desolation in her heart. She wanted to call him back, but knew he wouldn't come. She wanted to tell him it was all a mistake, she loved him, she wanted him—but she knew he would never believe her. He had gone back to Nadia instead. Nadia, who had been his mistress and still held more power over him than Philippa could hope to gain in a lifetime's marriage.

Slowly, moving as if each step were a separate agony, Philippa went back up the stairs. A dark pit of unhappiness had opened before her and she knew already that Zane had been right. Asking Kevin here was the last way to resolve her problems.

Kevin arrived at about ten o'clock the next morning. He looked a little less of the city businessman now, in linen slacks and a casual shirt, but he still didn't look comfortable against the setting of rocks and waves. He came rather doubtfully into the house, still clearly unsure of his welcome, and looked uncertainly at Philippa who had spent most of the night trying to think of ways to put him off and had finally mentally shrugged her shoulders and decided to let the fates do what they would.

The first awkward moment was, however, helped by Nadia, who came down the stairs at just that moment— by accident or design? Philippa wondered waspishly— and paused on the third step from the bottom, just where a beam of sunlight caught her at its most flattering.

'Hullo!' The low voice held a note of interest as she took in Kevin's appearance. 'A new arrival? Introduce me, Philippa.'

Once again Philippa was acutely conscious of the contrast between Nadia, in her silk shirt and slim-fitting trousers, both in a clear aquamarine that made her blonde hair look even paler, and herself in denims and an old shirt. But she would *not* try to compete, she told herself fiercely, and quelled an uncomfortable thought that she might in fact have dressed a little more carefully if Nadia *hadn't* been around.

'This is Kevin Brant,' she said tonelessly. 'Kevin, this is Nadia George, Zane's friend.'

'Nadia George?' Kevin came forward quickly and took the hand Nadia held out towards him. 'I thought I recognised you. I think I've seen just about everything you've done on TV. You were fantastic in that thing about the airline—I watched every episode. Mind you, I didn't think the script was all that it could have been. All those corny lines! Still, you were great.'

'Thank you.' Nadia came down the last three steps and smiled at him. 'We must have a long talk some time. But you'll excuse me now—Zane wants me in the study.' She glided past them and disappeared.

'Well!' Kevin exclaimed, looking after her. 'You never told me *she* was your other guest. When did she arrive? Isn't she a stunner! Even better off screen than on.'

'If you say so, I've never seen her.' Philippa was disconcerted by Kevin's obvious admiration for the actress and her voice was brusque as she said: 'Would you like to bring your case upstairs? Then we could walk round the island, if you like.'

'Mm, I suppose so.' Kevin followed her up the stairs. 'What do you do for kicks round here, Pippa? Walk round the island the other way? Honestly, I just don't see how you can live here without going raving mad. How about Nadia? Does *she* like it?'

'I've no idea.' Philippa opened a bedroom door and showed him in. 'She hasn't seen much of it. She seems to spend most of her time with Zane in his study.'

'Oh—like that, is it?' Kevin set down his suitcase and turned to her. 'I knew that guy would be no good to you, Pippa. I could see at a glance what he'd be like. I didn't expect to be proved right quite so soon—but it's just as well, isn't it? Now you can come back with me and everything will be the way it was before.'

No, it won't, Philippa thought. Nothing could ever be the way it was before. She'd been loved by Zane, however briefly, and that changed everything. Those hours—or minutes—in his arms had altered her whole life; and now that she was with Kevin again she could see just how far short of Zane he fell in her heart. There was no chance at all of their resuming the relationship that had seemed so happy in the crowded streets of Coventry. There was certainly no chance of her ever returning to the city—or even to the mainland.

'I'm sorry, Kevin,' she said quietly. 'I was wrong to ask you here. There isn't any future for us—there never was. I'll never leave Bethou, and if that means never leaving Zane—well, that's the way it'll be. This is where I belong.'

'Where you belong?' Kevin began to bluster. 'Now look, Pippa, I didn't give up a comfortable hotel to come and stay on this benighted island just to hear you say we've got no future. Where you belong, indeed— you belong with *me*, wherever I am—get that into your head! You belong——'

'I *don't*. Please, Kevin, don't let's quarrel again. I've said I was wrong—I was upset when I rang you—and I'm sorry. Please, let's forget it. Go back if you like and forget me too. Or else just finish your holiday here, and let's be friends. I don't want us to part on bad terms, Kevin.'

Kevin opened his mouth to protest again; then he glanced out of the window and his face changed. Philippa followed his glance and saw Zane and Nadia walking together along the shore.

'All right,' Kevin said thoughtfully, 'I'll do that, Pippa. I'll stay on here as your guest, and we'll see what happens.' There was a gleam in his eyes as he turned to his suitcase. 'Perhaps someone is going to get a surprise!'

# CHAPTER NINE

THE 'foursome' proved to be even more uncomfortable than the *ménage à trois*. Philippa was thankful that they were only to meet at mealtimes; that first lunch together was bad enough and she cast around in her mind for things to say, disconcerted by Zane's withdrawal, Nadia's mocking amusement and Kevin's barely concealed belligerence. It only needed one spark to set off an explosion, she thought uneasily.

'Kevin and I are going to walk round the island this afternoon,' she remarked, trying to ignore Kevin's less than enthusiastic response to this announcement. 'Anyone else like to come? I thought we might swim in Petit Bay.'

'*Petit* would have to be right,' Kevin observed, cutting himself some cheese. 'Nowhere on Bethou could be described as *grand*!'

Philippa threw him a quelling glance and caught Nadia's eye. The older girl raised fine eyebrows slightly and Philippa felt the colour come into her cheeks. Oh, why did they have to be there, the two of them? How could she and Zane ever hope to sort out their problems with other people around all the time—especially when the other people were Nadia and Kevin. She looked at Zane, but his face was impassive. Didn't he ever show his feelings? Or maybe he didn't have any to show. Maybe it was all a mask, even when he seemed to be at his most passionate.

The memory of his passion brought more warm colour to her cheeks and she hastily got up from the table and went to fetch some apples. And that was ironic, too. It had been easy for Eve—but Zane was no Adam and the mere offering of an apple wasn't going to win him round. But then nothing was, was it? His eyes as he looked at her were cold and hard, almost colourless, their brilliance faded. Obviously he was as fed up with the situation as she was.

154

A spark of defiance lit in her then. So he didn't care! All right—she would do as she liked, then. She turned to Kevin again and gave him her most dazzling smile.

'If you don't want to walk, then what about going over to Guernsey? I'll show you some of the places you haven't seen yet. I don't suppose you've seen everything. What about the Little Chapel?'

'Isn't there *anything* big around here?' Kevin demanded. 'No, I haven't seen the Little Chapel. What's so special about it, anyway? And what do we do after we've seen that?'

'Go somewhere else, I suppose.' Honestly, he wasn't co-operating at all! 'The cliffs around St Martin's are lovely. And we could have tea somewhere.' She smiled coaxingly at him. 'The Little Chapel is really rather fun. It's the smallest in the world——'

'You astound me!'

'—and it was built by a monk. It's decorated with shells and broken china.'

Kevin stared at her. 'Sounds terrific! All my life I've wanted to see a chapel decorated with broken china. And this is one of the attractions of Guernsey?'

'Yes, it is.' Philippa was growing angry now, especially when she caught Nadia's amused glance. 'You'll understand when you see it. Let's go, shall we?'

'Well, if it's a choice between walking round Bethou and visiting this chapel, I suppose I'd better agree.' Kevin got up with a martyred air. 'But the sooner I get you back to civilisation, the better I'll be pleased! This place eats into your brain, I'll swear it does!'

Philippa bit her lip. Really, Kevin was being deliberately awkward. What was he trying to do—engineer a row between her and Zane, between himself and Zane, or what? More than ever she wished she hadn't invited him. It was making things worse, just as Zane had predicted, and a quick look at her husband's stony face told her that there would be no help coming from that direction.

Once across the strand, Kevin recovered some of his good humour. He squeezed Philippa's hand, then slipped his arm round her waist and smiled at her.

'That's better! At least this is a bit nearer to civilisation. You must admit, Pippa, the facilities on Bethou are a bit on the short side.'

'Are they?' she returned coldly. 'It has all the facilities I want.'

'Oh, you're joking! There's just nothing there. I can't understand you, Pippa—I mean, you've lived on the mainland, you know what a city should be like——'

'Full of noise and pollution, with the chance of being mugged on every corner?' she enquired. 'That's civilisation? No, thanks, Kevin—I'll stick with Bethou. You may not be able to play Space Invaders there, but at least you're safe—from any kind of invader.'

'Oh yes? And what about the German Occupation during the last war?' Pippa was silent and Kevin looked triumphant. He led her to his car, parked near the Bethou garage, and unlocked the door. 'You see, it may be all very well being small, but sometimes big can be very useful too. Now—tell me the way to this Little Chapel—that's if you're determined to go there.'

Philippa's spirits rose a little when they reached the tiny building and Kevin nodded as if in unexpected pleasure at the colours of the thousands of shells and scraps of china that covered its walls. Together they explored it and marvelled at the amount of minute rooms and chapels within. Decoration was still going on in a few parts, but most of it was thickly encrusted with colourful pottery, much of it forming pictures and crosses on walls and ceilings. Kevin took several photographs and came out looking a great deal more satisfied than either of them had expected.

'Quaint,' he observed as they wandered down the track to look at the clock workshop. 'Very quaint indeed. Next time I break a cup, I'll donate it! Where now?'

Philippa glanced at her watch. 'Well, we could have tea somewhere. There are plenty of places. Or we could go back. I'd still rather like a swim.'

'We'll do both,' Kevin said indulgently. 'And then we'll come over again for dinner this evening. It's nice to get you on your own, Pippa. Like old times. It's what we've been needing.'

Philippa looked at him doubtfully. Hadn't she made it clear even now that she wouldn't be going back with him? But she supposed he thought that persistence would pay off. With a sigh, she said: 'Kevin, I can't come out to dinner with you. I'm married? I'm just not free——'

'Oh, that's rubbish,' he interrupted. 'Pippa, we've had all this out before. Your marriage isn't a marriage at all and you know it. Cut your losses, Pippa, and come back with me. You'll forget this place as soon as you're away from it. You did before, after all.'

'Please, Kevin,' she begged, 'don't let's go through all that again. I've told you—I'm sorry, but I made a mistake. It would never have worked for us. Be thankful that we found out in time.'

Kevin stared at her. His slightly plump face had hardened and his chin looked belligerent. 'I haven't found out anything,' he said slowly! 'Only that once you get an idea in your head there seems to be no shifting it. But that doesn't mean I have to give up trying.' He lifted a hand as she started once more to protest. 'All right, I won't say any more now. But believe me, Pippa, I *haven't* given up. I'll just try a different angle, that's all.'

He said no more as they found a tea-room and shared a pot of tea and a plate of scones, but Philippa was uneasy. Kevin was proving even more stubborn than she'd feared, and she wondered just what his 'new angle' might be.

She discovered it almost as soon as they got back to the island. Kevin entered the hall as if he were taking possession of a castle, marching through to Zane's study in obvious determination. He went so quickly that Philippa scarcely had time to protest, and flung open the door.

'Kendrick?' He stood on the threshold, breathing hard. 'I want a word with you.'

Timidly, Philippa came up behind him. She looked into the room and saw Zane there—Zane and Nadia,

together on the deep sofa. They were looking up at
Kevin in astonishment. Zane was slightly less immaculate than usual in cream linen slacks and shirt, his shirt
unbuttoned and his hair ruffled. Nadia, settling back
into the cushions at his side, lifted her hands and
deliberately fastened the buttons of her own silk shirt.

You didn't need to be Sherlock Holmes to guess what
they'd been doing, Philippa thought, and her heart
sank. Why was she bothering? Why was she clinging to
her marriage when it was so obviously a farce? All
right, Zane had made love to her and it had been like
flying, but it had clearly meant nothing at all to him.
Nadia had arrived the very same day and since then
he'd hardly spared Philippa a glance, except when they
were quarrelling. It would never be any different. Why
go on trying?

'It's usual to knock,' he was saying now to Kevin, his
tone deceptively mild. 'Or maybe you hadn't realised
that? I suppose it's different back in Coventry.'

Kevin's face reddened and he took a step into the
room. 'I haven't come to bandy words, Kendrick,' he
began. 'I've come to find out just how long you intend
playing out this charade. How long you intend keeping
Pippa here, chained to you——'

'I'm not keeping Philippa here at all. She stays of her
own free will. It *is* her home—hasn't she told you that?'

'Yes, she has, and she's told me too how you tricked
her into marriage with you, to keep it.' Philippa opened
her mouth to protest, but he swept on. 'I've never heard
of anything so disgustingly immoral in my life! It's—it's
positively medieval! Well, I'm not prepared to stand by
and see her life ruined for the sake of a house, and
you'd better understand that. I mean to take Pippa
back with me, where she belongs, and I think if you
were half a man you'd recompense her for what she'll
be losing here—the value of this house—and let her go
without any more fuss.'

'I've never made any fuss,' Zane returned, his voice
like ice, 'Nor have I seen any signs that Philippa wants
to go back. But perhaps she'd tell us herself.' His eyes
went past Kevin to Philippa, who was still in the

doorway, bewildered and angry at Kevin's high-handed action. She met Zane's eyes, her own wide and imploring. Oh, if only he would say he loved her, everything would be so simple, so easy! But her eyes went to Nadia, sitting at his side, so sleek and beautiful and self-assured, and she knew he never would.

'Well, Philippa?' Zane enquired silkily. 'What is it to be? A life of sophistication and civilisation in the fleshpots of Coventry? Or the rocks and the sea and the birds on Bethou?'

'Let's put it another way,' Kevin broke in harshly. 'A life of love with me—or emptiness with him?'

Philippa looked from one to the other. What were they doing to her? Between them, she felt like a fish on a hook, pulled this way and that. She looked again at Zane. If there were just a spark—just one glimmer of love for her in those cold eyes—but there was nothing.

'Perhaps I don't want either of those alternatives,' she said shakily, feeling she was really burning her boats now, that there would be no going back. 'Perhaps it's just Bethou I want—have always wanted. I've never made any secret of it—but your own oversized egos won't let you admit that any woman could want a house more than a man!'

Kevin turned and stared at her, and she felt a familiar exasperation. 'You needn't look so surprised,' she snapped. 'I've told you and told you. You should have listened in the first place.'

'She's right, you know.' Zane came to his feet. 'She never has made any secret of the fact that neither of us counts for a penny beside Bethou.' He came to the door in two strides and Kevin stepped aside, still looking dazed. 'Well, Philippa,' he said, looking down at her, his face now as cold and hard as marble, only his eyes showing a glitter of emotion, 'this seems to be it. You've made your wishes quite clear now. Later on, you may change, and if you do I'd be glad if you'll let me know. For the time being—well, we'll call it a day, shall we?'

He was past and up the stairs before she could speak, and as she stared after him Nadia got up more slowly, stretched herself and smiled.

'Well, you little fool,' she said to Philippa, lifting her blonde hair away from her neck, 'I hope you're satisfied. One of the most attractive men around and you blow it. My God, you'd even got him to *marry* you—and you *still* threw away every last chance you had!'

Philippa turned dulled eyes on her. Things were happening too fast, she didn't understand what it all meant. 'Chance?' she whispered. 'I never had a chance, not with Zane.'

Nadia snorted contemptuously. 'Of course you had a chance! You had more chances than I've had hot dinners! Weren't you alone here with him for over two months? Weren't you living in the same house for weeks after your wedding, before anyone else appeared on the scene? What was that but the biggest chance any girl could wish for? My God, you don't even know it when it comes along! Where have you been, for goodness' sake?'

'She's been with me,' said Kevin. 'She didn't need chances there. She knew how I felt.'

'And you didn't know how Zane felt?' Nadia's eyes glinted contempt. 'Philippa, you're just not real! Not in this day and age. Look, the man's head over heels about you, didn't you ever realise that? I saw it that first day—and I bet Kevin did too.'

Kevin looked uncomfortable. 'I didn't see any use in letting Pippa know if she didn't already,' he muttered. 'The man's no good to her, no good at all.'

'Well, I wouldn't like to express an opinion on that. In my experience Zane would be good for any woman.' Nadia's scornful eyes raked Philippa's slim body. 'But you don't even try! You seem to want to push him away, even though anyone can see that you're eating your heart out for him.'

'Anyone but the man concerned, perhaps,' Zane's voice came from the hall. 'No, Nadia, you're wrong there—Philippa cares only for her island, and as she said, it was only my ego that made me think otherwise.' His chilly gaze met Philippa's bewildered topaz eyes. 'All right, Philippa, you've got your way. I'll leave you to your island. You've made it very clear that that's what you want. If you need me, I'll be at the O.G.H. Not that I *expect* you to need me.' He turned to Nadia. 'Coming? We can collect your things later.'

Nadia threw Philippa a swift glance of triumph as she crossed to Zane's side. 'Of course I'm coming, Zane,' she murmured. 'I couldn't let you go alone, now could I?' She held out her hand to Kevin. 'We'll meet again, I hope. And remember—don't throw away too many chances. You may not get any more.'

Philippa, who had been standing rigid by the door, came to life suddenly. This couldn't be happening— Zane couldn't really be leaving her! She put out her hand and touched his sleeve, but he brushed her off as if she had been a fly. 'Goodbye, Philippa,' he said inexorably. 'Enjoy yourself on your island.' And without another glance he went on and out of the front door, closing it behind himself and Nadia with a firm, decisive click.

Philippa stared at the door, her head swimming. It must be a dream, it must! He would come back. He loved Bethou too. He couldn't leave it and her, just like that.

But the only sounds were those of the birds wheeling over the house, and she knew that Zane had already left the island. And there was a great empty ache where her heart had been.

Behind her, Kevin spoke and she jumped slightly— she'd almost forgotten he was there. 'It's for the best, Pippa—surely you can see that? You'll get over him and then we can make our own life together. We can sell this place—buy something really nice back home, start fresh. That's what you need, a new——'

Incensed, Philippa swung round on him. 'What I need?' she cried. 'How would *you* know what I need? You caused all this—you started it all! Now finish it— just go away, leave me alone, and don't ever come back—I don't want to see you again for the rest of my life!'

Kevin took a step towards her, his face still complacent, still so sure that he knew best. 'It's all right, Pippa,' he said comfortingly. 'I know just how you feel. Have a good cry, that's it—let it all out. I won't leave you, I——'

'Oh, for God's sake, *go*!' she screamed, lashing out wildly as he tried to take her in his arms. 'Go away—anywhere—back to Coventry, or to the North Pole if you'd rather. Can't you understand—*I just don't want you!* I've tried and tried not to hurt you and look where it's got me! Now just get out—and don't come back. You're bad news for me, Kevin, and I'm beginning to think that Vivien is well out of it!'

Kevin's arms dropped to his side. His expression was almost funny, but Philippa wasn't in a mood for laughing. Then he pulled himself together with an obvious effort, turned away and said stiffly: 'Very well, Pippa, if that's how you feel. Far be it from me to stay where I'm not wanted. Perhaps it would have been better if you'd made it clear at the start.'

'I thought I had,' Philippa sighed. 'I didn't realise you had to have it yelled at you before you'd listen. I'm sorry, Kevin—it's been a complete washout for you. But I can't help it.'

Kevin didn't reply. He went up the stairs and Philippa heard him moving about. After a little while he came down, carrying his suitcase.

'I'll say goodbye, then,' he said, still in that stiff, unnatural voice. 'I just hope you haven't made a terrible mistake, Pippa.' He held out his hand and Philippa shook it mechanically. 'Vicci will be disappointed,' he added in a last attempt to make her feel guilty. 'But still, we can't go through life pleasing other people all the time, can we?' He went out and shut the door.

Philippa leant her head against the wall. She felt utterly exhausted—and utterly alone. In just a few minutes she had lost both Kevin and Zane. Neither of them, she was sure, would ever come back.

Slowly, her feet dragging, she climbed the stairs to her bedroom. It looked cold and unwelcoming for the first time since she had known it. She opened the door into the room she had had decorated for Zane and

gazed for a long time at the tawny colours, the sheer
animal masculinity of the bed where she and Zane had
made love, covered with its sensuous fur bedspread.

All that was over. Now, she just had Bethou—and
wasn't that what she wanted?

The night dragged by. Philippa sat gazing sightlessly
from the window until it was too dark even to make out
the shadows of the main island. The air was cooler and
she shivered as she moved. She ought to have
something to eat, or at least a hot drink, but she didn't
have the energy to go downstairs and get it. More out
of habit than because she really wanted to, she
undressed and climbed into bed. But she didn't sleep; she
lay watching the regular brightness of the lighthouse and
going over everything in her mind, over and over again
until she wanted to scream, but her mind wouldn't stop;
it was like a long-playing record that went incessantly
back to the beginning as soon as it reached the end.

As dawn touched the sky she turned over restlessly
and wondered just why she was so unhappy. She had
what she wanted, didn't she? She had Bethou. That
would have been enough a few months ago—why
wasn't it enough now?

The answer was easy to find. Because since then she'd
met Zane; because she was in love with him. And beside
that, nothing else was really of any importance at all.

It wasn't Bethou she hadn't wanted to leave, to go
away with Kevin. It wasn't Bethou that kept her here,
so firmly attached to rock and sea. It was Zane.
Because home now was where Zane was, and without
him even Bethou was just a shell.

With a muffled groan, Philippa turned over and
buried her head in the pillow. If only she had known
before—she might have been able to come closer to
him, even perhaps, with time, to make him feel
something for her even though it might never be love.
Between them, they might have been able to built a life
based on their common tastes, which she already knew
were many, their love for Bethou and her love for Zane.
Wouldn't there have been a chance?

If there had, she'd thrown it away. Infuriated by

what she had seen as Zane's deception, she'd destroyed any chance there might have been of their making something of their marriage. Now he had gone—gone with Nadia—and it didn't take much imagination to see that they would have no trouble in making a life together. Nadia had more or less said so.

When the sun finally came up Philippa dragged herself from the bed and went into the bathroom. She looked into the mirror. Talk about death warmed up, she thought ruefully. Red-rimmed eyes with dark shadows all around them, puffy skin and lank hair. No wonder Zane had found it easy to leave her! She'd lost weight, too, due no doubt to all those missed meals, and her cheeks were thin and hollow.

Sighing, she switched on the shower and stood under it, hoping it would refresh her spirits as well as her body. The water drenched her skin and brought tired cells back to life, and she did feel a little better as she dried herself and went back to her room to dress. She hesitated over jeans and T-shirt, then bit her lip and deliberately chose a flowered skirt and a pretty blouse with an embroidered collar. Now that Nadia wasn't here there was no reason to compete—or not compete. And she really did feel she needed to do something to show the world that she hadn't been completely beaten.

Not that there was much world to be shown. The house was deathly quiet and there was no movement on the opposite shore. It was still too early for holidaymakers and the only signs of life were the seabirds picking their way along the weed-encrusted rocks on the shore.

Philippa wandered aimlessly from room to room. She looked into the study, where Zane's word-processor stood mute. He would have to come back for that, and for the rest of Nadia's things, she thought, but she had no hope that he would stay. He'd left her and that was final.

In the kitchen she made herself some toast and coffee. She still couldn't quite believe what had happened. It had all been so quick—as if some tight piece of elastic, holding them together, had finally snapped. It must have been stretching for some time—getting a little nearer to breaking-point with each quarrel, each crisis. And now that it had broken, that was the end. There was no way to mend elastic.

Upstairs again, she looked into her father's old room. It had been cleared of its furniture, but there was still quite a lot in there—boxes and trunks containing goodness knew what. Philippa dropped on her knees and opened one at random. All this would have to be got rid of, she thought, lifting out the heavy books that had been packed into it. She held one in her hands, turning it over curiously, staring at it before she remembered. Of course—the old diary, the one filled with that beautiful copperplate handwriting. Kept, she'd thought, by her grandfather or grandmother. She had meant to read it when she had first found it and had then forgotten.

Philippa straightened up and carried it through to her own room, where the sun shone warmly through the windows. She wasn't really interested now, but it might help to pass the time. And it might shed some light on that old quarrel, the one that had come down the generations to herself and Zane. She had an odd feeling that if it did, if she could only discover the truth, it just might help.

But when she opened it, she found it was not a diary after all. It was something that, to Philippa, was infinitely more valuable—an account, written by her grandmother, Philippe's second wife, of the quarrel between Philippe and his elder son, Raoul. It told too of the bitterness that old Philippe handed down to his second son. And as Philippa read the even, sloping handwriting, she found herself transported into another world; a world of Guernsey as it had been in the past, when few visitors came to roam the cliffs and beaches, when cars were rare and telephones owned only by the rich. In those days there had been an even closer community than there was today, even though distances had been, for practical purposes, greater. Everyone knew everyone else, or if they didn't they knew his sisters, his cousins and his aunts. In such a close community attitudes were bound to be different; and Philippa realised as she read that they should not be judged by today's standards. Families that were closer were bound to be more violently riven when a difference did arise. Small things mattered more when the larger events passed by.

Her grandmother was, as Philippa had judged from her pictures, sweet and gentle. The rift between husband and son had been a great distress to her. She had married Philippe because she had been a close friend of both him and his wife, Adele, and had promised her on her deathbed that she would care for the bereaved husband. Both women had known that, left alone, Philippe was liable to sink into depression; he was the kind of man who needed and relied upon his wife, and Philippa's eyes filled with tears as she read how Adele had begged Susan to take her place, and how gratefully Philippe had turned to her in his need.

But his son Raoul hadn't seen it that way. Grief-stricken at the loss of his mother, he had turned against his father and the woman who was to become his stepmother, raving and cursing in his pain. Philippa read how Susan had known that he would recover eventually, had begged Philippe to wait, to let the boy come round in his own time or, failing that, to make allowances for the idealistic young man's way of seeing everything in black and white. But Philippe wouldn't listen; he sent Raoul away and disinherited him by moving house, ignoring all the young man's obvious unhappiness and, later, the letters that came from the mainland where Raoul had gone.

Susan had known that both men were acting from the nature in which they were so alike, their judgement warped by grief. But she knew too that neither would either listen to reason or give way; their inborn obstinacy prevented it. Hoping that Raoul would make a happy life for himself, she had concentrated on looking after her husband, but all her love and care had not been enough to prevent the depression and bitterness—caused largely by guilt, Philippa guessed—that eventually overtook him—and which, tragically, he passed on to his son, Susan's only child and Philippa's father.

It was several hours before Philippa laid the book down, and she found that her cheeks were wet with tears. The sadness of its writer had come down to her across the years and she felt a sharp, poignant sympathy with the woman who had taken on her friend's husband and son and seen failure, not only with them, but with her own son as well. She must have died still regretting the obstinacy of the men she loved—for with all her trials, the love she had for them shone through every word.

Her last hope had been that the rift might be healed, late though it might be. But it never had; father and sons had died still angry, still bitter, and that was the greatest tragedy of all.

And even now, Philippa thought with a stab of guilt, the feud had been continued. She and Zane had clashed at the very beginning because of the quarrel between their fathers, a quarrel they didn't even know the truth of. What would Susan have made of it—a feud that went on even to the grandchildren? Philippa conjured up the picture of that sweet, kind face she remembered from pictures, and felt ashamed.

Well, that was one thing she could do. She could at least try to mend the old quarrel. She could take this book to Zane, tell him that she knew now that his father *had* been badly treated, had had every right to be angry, and that she, at least, was sorry. What they would do about Bethou, she didn't know; perhaps it would be the best thing after all if she allowed him to buy her share. He was at least morally entitled to the opportunity.

What she would do then, she hadn't the least idea. Because if Bethou wasn't a home without Zane, then neither would anywhere else be. So it didn't really matter where she went, did it—if Zane wasn't there too.

# CHAPTER TEN

IT was easier, Philippa found, to decide to do something than actually to do it. Having made up her mind to approach Zane and give him the book, she took several days to gather together the courage to cross to the main island and go to St Peter Port to do so. Mostly, she knew, her reluctance was the fear of rejection; after all, why should he accept her now when he had shown no inclination to do so before—in spite of Nadia's assurance that he was in love with Philippa, in spite of his tender lovemaking, she still couldn't quite believe that he had such feeling for her. Nadia might just have been trying to make her feel worse when he left her, rubbing salt into the wound. And as for his lovemaking—well, that was probably the way he behaved with any woman in bed.

She roamed about the tiny island, watching the sheep and the birds, picking her way across the rocks at low tide, swimming in the little bay at high tide. If she were to spend the rest of her life without Zane, she had to start learning how straightaway. But it was a hard lesson, and she lay awake at night wondering if she would ever learn it. The future stretched ahead as bleak as a wasteland, vast and empty.

At last she could put it off no longer. Her half-conscious hope that Zane would return, if only to collect his belongings, had ended when a strange taxi-driver arrived for Nadia's cases. Still she was tempted to do nothing, to wait, for surely he would come eventually. He'd been in the middle of a play; he would have to collect his script if nothing else. But she knew he was entitled to the truth, and that only she could tell him. There must be no more delay.

She dressed carefully. Nadia or no Nadia, she had to appear at her best, even if the other girl did overshadow her, in her designer dresses and expensive casuals.

Philippa had never been able to afford clothes like that, but she knew that she normally looked good enough in her own chain-store clothes. Her natural good taste helped her to choose things that would co-ordinate and she often put together separates that achieved a far more elegant-looking effect than could have been expected.

Today, her full black and white skirt, teamed with a *broderie anglaise* blouse and red belt, looked fresh and pretty. She flicked a comb through her cap of rich brown hair, noticed that she had lost so much weight lately that her belt needed another hole in it, then picked up her bag. The book was slipped inside, together with sandals for putting on once she had crossed the causeway, and she was ready.

In a few hours, she would know. She would have faced Zane again, talked with him, given him the account written by her grandmother. And—perhaps—she would have been able to read the truth in his face. Perhaps she would know whether or not he cared for her—or whether their marriage had, after all, been nothing but a charade.

The journey across the island took longer than she expected. There was no car at her disposal now and she didn't want to call on Tommy's taxi—already she had had some difficulty in fending off Hubert and Margaret's curiosity as to where Zane had gone, particularly as she had been left all alone. Her replies that he had gone to do some research for his new play had left them unsatisfied; why hadn't he taken her with him? And why had he gone immediately after having guests, when the sudden emptiness might leave her lonelier than ever? Philippa's repeated assurances that she wasn't at all lonely, she loved Bethou too much ever to be lonely there, had been received with unconvinced looks and sniffs, and she knew that it wouldn't be long before more questions were asked: when was Zane coming back, and so on. She sighed. It was nice having two people like Hubert and Margaret, so close and concerned for her, but it could certainly be very awkward at times.

However, neither Hubert nor his wife were about when she crossed and she set off up the lane to the bus stop with a sigh of relief. It would never do for them to find out that she was going to the Old Government House—from that piece of information it would be a short route indeed to the truth that Zane—and Nadia— were staying there. And Philippa wasn't ready yet for anyone to know that her marriage had gone so disastrously wrong.

Buses were erratic on this route and Philippa wasn't at all sure when one would come along, but after she had been waiting for a while it appeared and she climbed aboard, nodding and smiling at the passengers she knew but thankful that there were no seats near them where she would feel obliged to sit. Instead, she squeezed herself on to the back seat, beside some holidaymakers, and spent the journey gazing out of the window. She was feeling slightly sick, her anxiety throbbing painfully through her head, and conversation was something she just couldn't have coped with.

The bus bumped along the narrow, leafy lanes. Philippa stared out, automatically watching the scenery, identifying the different districts, glancing at houses she knew. She wondered just where she would be when this chaotic situation was eventually sorted out, the tangle of her life unravelled. If it ever was. Would she still be on Guernsey, living the life she loved among people she had grown up with and understood? Or would she follow her uncle, Zane's father, into exile, living—or existing—on the mainland, eating her heart out for what she had left behind?

At last the bus turned down the final hill into St Peter Port and people began to gather up bags and baskets. The harbour glittered below them, the masts of the yachts in the marina dancing in a ballet of their own. Castle Cornet lay white and serene above the harbour. Holidaymakers wandered along the quays in bright clothing, locals sat on boats in shabby guernseys, their faces tanned by the sun and the salty air. There was a pleasant air of bustle, without hurry. Things would happen, but in their own time. Nobody was going to rush them.

Philippa left the bus and made her way to the Old Government House. Her heart was thumping and the sick feeling had returned. In a few minutes she could be face to face with Zane. He might, of course, be out—but in that case she would simply wait until he returned. She was determined now to complete her mission, even if it did end in nothing.

The reception area was quiet when she went in. A small family—young couple and two pleasant-looking children—went through, smiling at her, and she looked at them with envy. In different circumstances, that could have been herself and Zane. But she doubted if it ever would. She knew now that she wasn't already carrying Zane's child—his heir. The knowledge had come with mixed feelings; she didn't know whether to be glad or sorry. It was probably just as well, looked at from a purely practical point of view. But she regretted that image of a tiny, dark-haired baby with sapphire blue eyes. . . .

As she glanced around for a receptionist, she heard a movement and a hiss of indrawn breath. Startled, she turned quickly—and saw Nadia, coming down the stairs and gazing at her.

'*You!*' It was no more than a whisper. 'What are *you* doing here?'

'I came to see Zane.' Philippa kept her voice steady, determined not to let the other girl gain the upper hand. 'Is he here? I'll wait if not.'

'You'll wait a long time, then.' The other girl's voice was tinged with malice. 'He's not here. He left—three days ago.'

'Three days ago?' That must have been almost as soon as he'd left Bethou! 'But—where did he go?'

'Why ask me?' The bitterness chilled the air between them. 'Look, you'd better come up to my room. I don't intend to talk here.'

Bewildered, Philippa followed her. She had expected Zane to be here, with his mistress—yet it seemed that he'd spent no longer than one night in the hotel. Why? What had gone wrong between them? She'd thought Nadia held all the cards.

Nadia led her to a luxuriously-furnished bedroom, shut the door and faced her. Over her shoulder, Philippa could see signs of packing: a suitcase open on the bed, clothes strewn around. So Nadia was leaving too. Where was she going—to join Zane?

'I don't understand,' she began. 'I thought——'

'You think too much,' Nadia snapped. 'And you don't understand enough. You never understood Zane—never! Yet because of you—oh, what's the use? You won't understand if I tell you now.' She shrugged away and picked up a dress. 'Women like you ought to be banned,' she said over her shoulder. 'You wreck everything for the rest of us.'

'Would you mind telling me what you're talking about?' Philippa asked, her bewilderment growing, and Nadia swung round again.

'You see! You haven't the faintest idea, have you! You just don't even begin to see that you've got Zane— *Zane Kendrick*—in such a state he hardly knows what he's doing. You don't even realise you've only got to crook your little finger and he'll come running. You haven't an inkling that he'd throw up everything for you, if you gave him even the smallest sign that you cared. No—all you care about is your bloody island, and nobody's ever cared more for a few smelly rocks than for Zane Kendrick before. Maybe it's a new angle; maybe I ought to try it myself.'

Philippa stared at her. Her head spun. It couldn't be true—none of it was true. She shook her head, trying to clear it, but the thoughts still chased around inside like ants disturbed in their anthill.

'Look, you've got it all wrong,' she said. 'Zane doesn't care about me. He only married me for Bethou. Oh, it's a complicated story, but it's true. It was a marriage of convenience for both of us.' She blinked, thinking how quickly it had become something very different for her. 'He doesn't love me,' she went on, her voice wobbling. 'He never did. He never gave the slightest sign of it.'

'No, well, he wouldn't,' Nadia remarked indifferently. 'That's always been one of Zane's principles. Never let yourself care. Only this time he seems to have forgotten it. It's still hard for him to show, though.'

'What do you mean? Why should that be his principle?'

Nadia turned and glanced at her. She seemed to be thinking, weighing up whether to say more. Then she gave a tiny shrug and turned back to her packing.

'You obviously don't know a lot about Zane,' she said coolly. 'About his early life, I mean. You don't know, for instance, that his mother left him and his father when Zane was only five years old.'

The information hit Philippa like a blow. She sat down. 'No, I didn't know that. Zane never told me.' All that talk about his father and he'd never told her that! Why? It must have been one of the most important events of his life.

'He doesn't tell anyone. I only know because my family have known Zane since he was a small boy. And because I've watched him for a long time. Zane never gets close to a woman, he just doesn't trust them. If he married you for convenience, that explains a lot. He probably thought it would keep him safe from danger—the danger of love. If he fell in love with you afterwards, he must have gone through his own peculiar kind of hell.'

'Yes.' Philippa stared unseeingly at the carpet. A shaft of pity pierced her for the little boy who had loved and lost his mother so young, and who had grown up to be wary and distrustful of all women. No wonder he found it hard to give his heart; he was constantly afraid of rejection and betrayal.

And Philippa had given him no sign that she would be any different. She had taken pleasure in his lovemaking—and then she had run away, rejected his attempts at reconciliation and invited her old boy-friend to stay! How must he have felt? she wondered, and an agony of remorse twisted her heart. There had been so much bitterness in Zane's life, and she was adding to it.

No wonder he had left her. He must have had all that he could take.

'Why are you telling me this?' she asked quietly.

'God knows! Not because I think it'll help, that's for sure!' The actress looked at her, eyes gleaming with dislike. 'I wouldn't help you to cross the road! Zane and I were getting along fine until you came on the scene. Oh, I knew marriage wasn't likely to be on the cards—but anything else was, and you never know what might happen. Anyway, I'm not in the market for wedding bells myself—my career's too important to me. And Zane was doing good things for me there, too. He was writing his new play for me, you know. Now I don't even know if he's going to finish it.' She crammed the last garment into the case and closed it with a snap. 'That's it. Now I'm going. Back to London—away from this dump. Guernsey's been nothing but bad news for me, and I guess Zane's feeling the same—wherever he is.'

'But haven't you *any* idea?' Philippa asked desperately. 'I thought he was going to stay with you—what happened?'

Nadia's eyes were hard. 'I thought that too. But it didn't work out—and I've told you why. Because of you, little Philippa, that's why! I could see the way it was going to be from the start. Oh, I tried, believe me—but it was never on. And when he left, he just left. No word. He could be in Timbuctoo, San Francisco or on the moon for all I know.'

She lined up her cases by the door and lifted the telephone to summon a porter. Philippa looked helplessly at her back. Nadia wouldn't say any more, she knew that. She probably regretted having said so much. Not that it was any help to Philippa, any of it. Not if Zane had disappeared so completely.

Slowly she made her way to the door, hesitating on the threshold. Nadia had moved away and was staring out of the window. She wouldn't welcome a conventional goodbye; her stiff, suede-clad back was as expressive as her face and Philippa knew that she would neither turn nor reply. Silently, she turned away and left the room.

So that was that, she thought, coming out again into the bright sunshine. Zane had vanished and even Nadia didn't know where he was. According to her he was in a 'state' over Philippa herself—something Philippa still found hard to believe. But it didn't seem likely that the actress would have said so if it really wasn't true—or if she thought that there was any chance of Philippa meeting Zane again. Nadia wasn't that generous—no, she'd told Philippa because she wanted her to suffer even more, not because she wanted to help.

Slowly, her throat aching with the tears that she would not be able to shed until she reached Bethou, Philippa walked down the hill, hardly noticing the throngs of people who crowded the pavements and wandered along the traffic-free precincts.

They were happy, these people, she thought. No cares, no worries, nothing to think about at all except enjoying themselves. They would go back to their hotels later and delicious meals would be placed in front of them, and then they would go to bed to sleep peacefully before spending another carefree day tomorrow. No bad dreams would mar their slumbers, no regrets or remorse keep them awake. Everything in their world was fine.

Don't be stupid, her inner voice told her sharply. Stupid and selfish. Of *course* everyone isn't happy, of course they have worries and problems. Did Philippa think she was the only one whose life seemed to be going awry? Did she truly believe that none of those apparently cheerful faces hid agony or despair? Really, it was about time she stopped feeling so sorry for herself and started to face reality. She'd made a mess of things, yes? Then there were only two things to do—put right as much as she could and then get on with life as it was. Self-pity was something she couldn't afford. Look what it had done to her father—and her grandfather. Did she want to end up like them, a recluse on Bethou, empty and embittered?

Biting her lip, Philippa continued on down the street to reach the Town Church. Here there was even more activity and, glancing around at the crowds, she realised

that it was Thursday—the day on which the Market
was held and the traders wore traditional costumes to
sell their wares under gaily-striped awnings in the street.

Vaguely, more because she didn't know what else to
do than because she had a real interest, she turned and
wandered through the chattering bustle, only half seeing
the copper, glassware, candles and paintings. People
were looking eagerly for the flaws, some of them too
minute to be found, in a rack of guernseys being sold as
'seconds', and with a stab she thought of Zane,
handsome in his own navy guernsey on the morning
he'd found her in the car. And after that—a shudder of
mixed emotion, desire and longing and bitter loss shook
her body and she had to stop to regain her control. A
passing couple gave her a curious glance and hesitated,
as if to offer help, then passed on as she pulled herself
together and gave them an apologetic smile.

This was no good—no good at all. There was nothing
for her to do but return to Bethou, where at least she
could lick her wounds in private and begin to overcome
this dreadful self-pity that still threatened to overwhelm
her. That inner voice was right—it was damaging, even
destroying, and she had to fight it.

But she couldn't face that bus journey again. This
time it would have to be a taxi. And she turned on her
heel and went back towards the church to the cul-de-
sac, where the taxis waited.

Fortunately, Tommy wasn't there. It wouldn't really
have mattered, since it was only her arrival at the Old
Government House that Philippa hadn't wanted
known, but all the same she was relieved that she could
travel anonymously with a driver she didn't know. She
sat back and closed her eyes, trying to relax her body,
wishing that she could stop the thoughts that still
teemed like busy ants through her exhausted mind.
Zane—Kevin—Nadia—Zane: they moved restlessly
before her, their faces accusing, Zane's heartbreaking.
Had he really loved her? she wondered for the
thousandth time. Could they really have made that life
together that had seemed to her like an unattainable
Paradise? Was it all her fault that they weren't—her

fault for being insensitive, too absorbed in herself, too unforgiving over that old and futile quarrel?

Well, if it was, she would never know now. It was too late for her, too late for them both. Zane's patience had finally snapped and she had a strong feeling that once he had made up his mind there would be no turning back. No turning back—to her.

A tear crept out from under her closed eyelid and slipped slowly down her cheek. But there were no more to follow it; Philippa's heart was aching too much for tears.

Bethou looked small and remote when they finally arrived. Few people were about now; it was the hour when most holidaymakers would be looking for tea, or perhaps making their way back to hotels and apartments to put small children to bed. She thought of families together, young couples with children, laughing and relaxed as they enjoyed their holiday. They would remember Guernsey with pleasure and delight, and as she pulled herself together and paid the taxi-driver she reminded herself sharply that there was to be no self-pity—and hoped that pleasure and delight would indeed be all that those unknown visitors remembered Guernsey for. It was a happy island, and her own pain was something private.

The causeway was still clear enough to cross and she made her way through the rocks, aware of the weight of the book in her bag. She was sorry she hadn't been able to give it to Zane—but perhaps there would be another chance. There had to be—there were still most of his belongings on Bethou, including his play-script and word-processor. Even if he sent for them, as he'd done for Nadia's clothes, she could still give him the book by putting it into his own collection. One day he would find it—and know why she'd sent it.

She came to the shelving beach and walked the last few yards to the garden door, then hesitated, almost reluctant to go in. It was a different world in there and she wasn't sure that she wanted to enter it. She'd determined to keep self-pity and bitterness at bay—but would that be possible in this house that had seen so much of both? Wouldn't they seep out of the stones and surround her, eating into her own nature and——

The door swung slowly open. Philippa felt a great tremor pass over her body. She watched, her heart jerking painfully against her ribs; and then the world slipped away from under her feet and she felt herself swing wildly, uncontrollably, through a great empty void.

'Zane. . . .' she breathed, and her body crumpled.

## CHAPTER ELEVEN

THE room was dark when Philippa opened her eyes. She blinked painfully and tried to focus on a series of blurred images; furniture that looked peculiar, familiar yet strange, colours that were dimmed. And Zane. Zane with his face set in lines she'd never seen before, lines that in anyone else she would have identified as anxiety, tenderness, love. . . .

Slowly her vision cleared and she tried to sit up, but Zane pushed her back on soft cushions with a strong, gentle hand. She realised that the oddness of the furniture was due to the angle from which she was seeing it; she'd never lain just here before, on this particular couch. Her mind returning to normal, the distortion disappeared, and when she glanced up at Zane again she saw that he was now looking grim.

'Zane?' she whispered, and his eyes met hers, cold and angry.

'What in hell have you been doing to yourself, Philippa?' he demanded harshly. 'You're as thin as a rake, you weigh nothing. Haven't you been feeding yourself? What's Margaret been thinking of, hasn't she been cooking for you?'

'No—I told her I could manage. Zane, I don't need cooking for—I've been looking after myself for years, I——'

'It's a wonder there's anything left of you, then!' He

slipped his fingers into her waistband. 'Look at this!'
That *fitted* you a few weeks ago—now it's at least a size
too big. Have you been eating anything at all? Did you
eat today? Yesterday?'

Philippa tried to remember. Coffee, she'd had coffee
today—but yesterday? A couple of apples, she
remembered those—she gave up the struggle and
attacked instead.

'Well, you don't look so hot yourself! Your face is as
gaunt as a skeleton and you need a shave—or have you
decided to grow a beard? Maybe I'm not the only one
who's stopped caring!'

Zane stared at her, then he put up a hand and touched
his chin, almost exploringly, looking vaguely surprised
at the roughness beneath his fingers. He grinned
ruefully. 'Maybe you're right at that. Let's strike a
bargain, shall we? Suppose we both make ourselves
look a bit more respectable—though I must admit
there's nothing wrong with *your* appearance that a few
good square meals wouldn't put right—and then we'll
start again, hm? I think we have some talking to do
before I go back to the main island.'

Philippa looked up at him. Suddenly she knew that
she didn't want him to go, not even to shave. It didn't
matter if he looked like a broomhead, he had to stay
here with her, at least until the truth was out between
them.

'No,' she said quietly, and she put her own hand up
and touched that darkly shadowed chin. 'Don't go,
Zane. I—I've got something for you. I've just been over
to the hotel—the O.G.H.—to give it to you, only Nadia
said you'd gone. I never expected to find you here.'

'I came to see you,' he said simply, and she knew
then that there was hope. 'But, Philippa, you don't have
to——'

He stopped as she twisted round on the sofa and
found the bag he'd brought in with her. She rummaged
in it and drew out the book; the book that had been
written by her grandmother, the woman who had taken
the place of Zane's grandmother and become the
unwitting cause of so much trouble. She saw his eyes on

it, creased with a puzzled frown, and she handed it to him without a word.

'I don't understand,' Zane said slowly, turning it over in his hands. 'What is it, Philippa? Tell me.'

'You can read it all there,' she said steadily. 'It tells about the quarrel. It tells the truth—how your father was sent away and disinherited. It wasn't his fault, Zane, I know that now. Perhaps it wasn't anyone's fault. Perhaps bitterness was in their nature. Perhaps it's been in mine too—but I don't want that, Zane. Whatever there is between us, I don't want bitterness. That's why I brought you the book—that and because I thought you ought to know what really happened.'

Zane closed the book and laid it aside. His eyes were intent as he looked down at Philippa, and his mouth was grave. Her heart quickened as she met his gaze. There was hope, yes—but it wasn't going to be easy.

'Just what are you saying, Philippa?' he asked, his voice low and deep. 'Explain to me—in words of one syllable. I don't want any chance of further misunderstanding.'

Philippa took a deep breath. She didn't want to explain, she wanted Zane to understand without words. But he was entitled to all the explanation he wanted—and she remembered again his instinctive mistrust of women, born from the mother who had left him when he still depended on her. Somehow she had to prove that here was a woman he *could* trust. It was her only chance.

'I wanted you to know the truth,' she said simply. 'And I wanted you to know that *I* know it—and accepted it. My grandfather was wrong, Zane. I suppose we'll never know why—something in his own past, perhaps. How far do these things go back? But he was desperately unhappy when his first wife—your grandmother died. And his second—*my* grandmother— married him because she'd been a close friend of them both and knew that if he didn't have a wife he would quickly become so depressed that he wouldn't want to go on living. Your father, Raoul, couldn't understand that—he was too young and he was wrapped up in his own grief. But instead of giving him time, our grandfather lost his temper and turned the boy out. The bitterness started from there, for both of them.'

She paused. Zane tapped the book gently and said: 'And this?'

'It's an account of the quarrel and what happened afterwards. She never wanted it, Zane. She died still longing for a reconciliation.' Philippa stopped. Zane's eyes were on her, intent but veiled. He wasn't going to give her any help, beyond listening. 'I thought,' she want on in a low voice, 'that it might not be too late yet for that reconciliation, Zane. Grandmother wouldn't know about it—but we would. We'd know that the quarrel had been made up.'

'And is that what you want?' His eyes were still shadowed, unreadable. Philippa nodded, feeling the moisture in her own. She bit her lip to stop the tears.

'Yes, Zane, I want it.' She raised her eyes bravely to his, knowing that it had to be said and that she must be the one to say it—she, after all, had been the one who had done the rejecting. 'I want to start again,' she said quietly. 'I want a chance to make something of our life together. But if that isn't what you want, then I'll go away. I'll leave you in peace and I won't bother you again.'

'And Bethou?' he asked. 'What about Bethou? Don't you want it?'

'I don't want Bethou if I can't have you too,' she said. 'You see, I love you, Zane. And without you, Bethou is empty.'

Zane stared at her for a long moment. Outside she could hear the sounds of wind and tide rising together—a summer storm by the sound of it. Soon, Bethou would be cut off again, the sea surging between the two islands, and her stomach twisted at the thought that Zane would have to spend the night here.

She looked up into his eyes again and there was a strange, unfathomable expression in them. She didn't know what it was, what emotion it expressed. It was as if something inside were changing as she watched; as if some indefinable barrier were being torn down at last, after years of keeping enemies at bay. But was she an enemy? She shivered suddenly.

'Just say that again, Philippa,' he requested at last, and his voice was strange too. 'Just those last two sentences.'

A great surge of happiness pulsed through Philippa then as she knew without doubt that she was winning— had won. She lifted her arms and linked them behind his neck, drawing the shadowed face down to hers, and laid her cheek alongside his, not even noticing the bristles that rubbed her soft skin. 'I love you, Zane,' she murmured into his ear. 'Without you, Bethou is empty. *I love you.*' And then her control deserted her and she gripped him tightly, groaning out the words over and over again, letting them flow from her heart to his, kissing his face as she repeated it—'I love you, Zane, I *love* you'—wanting to say more but knowing that no other words would do, knowing that these were the only ones he wanted to hear.

His arms were round her too now, and they lay clasped tightly together, not wanting anything more at that moment but to feel each other close, to experience again the touching of two warm bodies that moulded to each other as if they had been built to fit. Zane was groaning too, muttering incoherently and rubbing his rough cheeks against hers, his hands roving over her body, his lips moving over her skin as he whispered, exploring her face and hair as if in a blind search for reassurance. Between them, they must have said the word 'love' a hundred times; at last they relaxed and lay, still close together, temporarily exhausted.

'I thought I'd never hear you say that,' he murmured at last, his fingers still twining through her short hair. 'I'd given up all hope. I thought that morning when we made love was all a dream and it would never happen again.'

'Did you love me then?' She knew the answer, but she wanted to hear it. She felt him nod.

'I loved you from the first moment I saw you.' His lips smiled against her breast. 'Lying there in the narrow berth on the ship—you looked adorable, so defenceless and so indignant. I wouldn't admit it, of course—that's why I was so furious—but afterwards I kept seeing that picture of you and wishing it could have been different. And then, when I found out who you were——'

'You knew, then?'

'I was pretty certain, as soon as you told me your name.' He hesitated. 'That's why I didn't tell you mine, of course. I couldn't risk making things worse. I wanted to tell you—but I was too afraid of losing you. You made it pretty clear what you thought of my side of the family, and I realised that once you knew who I was you'd give me short shrift. It was short enough as it was!' he added with a grin.

'But didn't you feel the same—about me? After the way your father had been treated?' Philippa thought of that visit made to Bethou when Zane was a small boy, before she'd been born. Already burdened with the feeling that he was unwanted, the less than welcoming reception he and his father had been given must have chilled the child even more. And it wasn't long after that that her father married in an attempt to sire his own heir to Bethou—and found himself a widower with a baby daughter.

'No, I didn't feel like that. It's an old quarrel, Philippa, and nothing to do with either of us. It didn't matter to me, except in as much as I'd made my father a promise, that I'd come back and claim Bethou if I could. I don't even know how seriously I meant to keep that promise—I might easily have just gone away again and considered it fulfilled. But then I saw you and I knew that you went with Bethou. I wanted you—and I could only get you, it seemed, by making Bethou seem the prime importance. So I was glad to take the chance.'

'Then you don't love Bethou after all?'

Zane's eyes softened. 'Oh yes, I do. I love it very much. But I loved you first, Philippa my darling—and I always will.'

Philippa sighed and snuggled closer. His warmth and solidity filled her with a calm certainty that from now on everything would be all right. But there was still one thing she had to know.

'And—Nadia?' she asked softly, her lashes hiding the expression in her eyes.

'Nadia?' Zane gave a short laugh. 'Well, there's not much point in my trying to hide Nadia from you, is there? Yes, Nadia and I had a pretty close relationship at one time—physically, that is. There was never any more than that in it. And we both knew it. It finished, I may tell you, quite a few years ago.'

'A few *years* ago?' Philippa digested this. 'But why did she come? And—Zane, I'm not saying I don't believe you, but when I passed the study I heard—well, I heard things about me. About not having to worry, you'd sort it out, it had all been a big mistake. And when Kevin walked in on you, you looked——'

Zane lifted his head and gave a shout of laughter. It was gusty, healthy, cleansing laughter, and Philippa stared up at him, wanting to laugh too but too bewildered. Zane looked down at her and controlled himself, but he was still grinning as he answered her.

'Oh, my poor Philippa! If only I'd known—but no, darling, it was nothing like that. Look, you knew I was writing a play. That play was for Nadia. She was to star in it—and that's why she came over. So that she could work through the part with me. So that I could get every word, every nuance, exactly right for *her*. Those things you heard us saying—they were lines from the play. I'll run it through the word-processor if you like— you can read it right there on the screen. And that day when Kevin walked in on us and caused all that trouble, for which I'll gladly flatten him if he ever shows so much as a toenail around here again—well, we just hadn't been able to get it right that afternoon. We'd both been working pretty hard—I suppose we probably did look a bit dishevelled, but it wasn't what *you* thought, my suspicious little wife!'

Philippa blushed deeply. Zane was regarding her with amusement, but in her heart she knew that she ought to have trusted him. She hadn't known that he loved her even then—but he'd married her. And she knew that

Zane was a man of integrity. As long as he was married to one woman, other relationships would be out.

'I'm sorry, Zane,' she whispered. 'I should have known—but I was so unhappy——'

'Unhappy? Why? Did you know that you loved me even then, Philippa?'

'I knew that morning—when you found me in the car. But it was there before—I don't know how long. Perhaps from the beginning, like you, only I wouldn't admit it. But when Nadia came and I thought there was no hope——' she shuddered and Zane gathered her close and laid his lips on hers.

'I think we've talked enough now, don't you?' he murmured, his voice rough with desire. 'It's time we gave our voices a rest and let our bodies have a chance. They know what to do, Philippa—they know what we need.' He drew her up into his arms. 'Shall we go upstairs?'

Together, arms twined about each other's waists, they went up the stairs and into the tawny bedroom where they had first made love. Philippa blinked to find that it was still light and realised that Zane had drawn the curtains downstairs when she had fainted. He drew these now and a dim gold light filtered into the room. The rich shades of the rug that lay across the bed seemed to welcome them with a sensuality that called to the need in them both, and Philippa stood submissively, her blood racing with an excitement that would soon transmit itself to her limbs and every muscle of her body, as Zane slowly and caressingly undressed her, his hands lingering on her soft skin and waking a response that had her shuddering with passion.

Suddenly she was trembling with impatience and her fingers shook as she undid his own buttons and slipped his shirt away from the broad shoulders. Then, with a smile, he checked her and laid her gently on the bed. She felt that familiar ache, low down, as she moved against the sensuous fur and watched Zane come to her, naked now, his yearning for her apparent in every hard line of his body. And then he was beside her, his length against hers, their bodies touching, skins and limbs and

lips mingling and merging in a wild drumbeat of
passion that had them whirling in a storm of their own,
and the blood beating in Philippa's ears sounded wilder
than any waves beating on rocks outside as Zane's
sensitive fingers played on her body as a musician plays
on a violin, bringing her through all the movements,
from the soft tenderness of a slow passage through an
increasing crescendo of mounting sensation to a final
crashing climax that had them both breathless and
crying out in each other's arms. All thought ceased and
instinct took over, guiding each movement with the
certainty of a millennium of experience, bringing to
each of them sensations and a depth of emotion as old
as time and as fresh as next year's spring. And when at
last it was over and they lay quietly together, their
bodies almost boneless, the sweetness was more piercing
than any agony, filling them both with a wonder that
anyone could experience it and live.

'It *is* all right now, isn't it?' Philippa whispered at
last. 'We won't go wrong again? We won't lose each
other?'

'Not if I have anything to do with it.' Zane's hands
moved possessively over her. 'And you'll be surprised at
the lengths I'm prepared to go to, to make sure. I've
already ordered the ball and chain! There'll be no more
inviting old flames to stay whenever you feel a little
piqued.'

Philippa kissed him quickly. 'I'm sorry about that,
Zane. It was unforgivable.'

'It wasn't, because I've forgiven you—but don't push
your luck!' He bit her ear gently. 'This wolf has very
sharp teeth—all the better to *eat* you with, my dear!'
There was a short silence and then he added more
seriously: 'No, Philippa, nothing's going to go wrong.
Not as long as we're always honest with each other and
don't harbour grudges. We've both seen what that can do.'

They lay quietly for a long time, talking softly,
exploring each other's minds as they had so recently
explored each other's bodies. Then Philippa said in a
tone of wonder: 'Do you know something, Zane? I'm
hungry!' and he laughed.

'I'm not a bit surprised! I don't think you've eaten properly for days. Let's have something to eat—what's in the kitchen?'

'Eggs, cheese, a bit of salad. Nothing much, I'm afraid.'

'Cheese omelette and salad, then. And while you're getting it, I'll shave.' He glinted a wicked look at her. 'Wouldn't do to go to bed with my lady wife in this unshaven state!'

'Your lady wife,' Philippa told him severely, 'would go to bed with you if you had a beard down to your toes. But don't grow one—it would get awfully in the way!' She reached for her clothes. 'I'll see you downstairs—with or without bristles!'

It was some time later when they finally pushed aside their plates and wandered out through the garden door to the clutter of rocks that stood like a gaunt black castle against the evening sky. The sudden brief summer storm had passed, leaving the sun low on the horizon; a great orange globe, its fire spreading over the dusky sky, turning the wisps of cloud that still signified a wind, somewhere high, to a deep tangerine. The sea, filling the strand between Bethou and Guernsey, was the colour of burnished copper and its glow reflected in Zane's and Philippa's faces as they stood gazing at their little kingdom.

'Shall we stay here, Philippa? Would you like that?' Zane whispered as he held Philippa in front of him, his arms linked across her breasts, tilting her body lightly back against his.

Philippa leaned her head back against his shoulder, revelling in the breadth and strength of it. A shoulder you could rely on , she thought dreamily, and wondered just what had kept them apart for so long. It seemed crazy now; trivial and crazy. Even Kevin had seen that they were meant for each other. But Kevin was far away now, far away from her thoughts and her heart. She hoped he would find happiness, but he was no longer her concern.

'I'd like to stay here,' she answered, 'if that's what you'd like too. But I told you, Zane—without you it's empty. Just a shell; a rather sad shell.'

'Then we'll fill it.' He swung her round to face him and his eyes laughed into hers. 'We'll fill it with love and laughter and happiness. And when the time comes, we'll fill it with Ozannes too—little ones, who'll grow up to love it as we do. And maybe one day care for it as we will.'

Philippa felt a leap of excitement as she looked at him, then pressed herself close against him. As a recipe for life, it sounded just about perfect.

'Let's go in,' she said, tucking her arm close into his. 'Let's go home.'

They took one last, lingering look at the blazing sky; then they turned and walked back down the grassy slope to where the grey granite house lay waiting for them. A new life was about to begin; a new era. For Zane and Philippa. For the Ozanne family. And for Bethou.

# 4 BOOKS FREE
## Enjoy a Wonderful World of Romance...

Passionate and intriguing, sensual and exciting. A top quality selection of four Mills & Boon titles written by leading authors of Romantic fiction can be delivered direct to your door absolutely FREE!

Try these Four Free books as your introduction to Mills & Boon Reader Service. You can be among the thousands of women who enjoy six brand new Romances every month PLUS a whole range of special benefits.

- Personal membership card.
- Free monthly newsletter packed with recipes, competitions, exclusive book offers and a monthly guide to the stars.
- Plus extra bargain offers and big cash savings.

There is no commitment whatsoever, no hidden extra charges and your first parcel of four books is absolutely FREE!

Why not send for more details now? Simply complete and send the coupon to MILLS & BOON READER SERVICE, P.O. BOX 236, THORNTON ROAD, CROYDON, SURREY, CR9 3RU, ENGLAND. OR why not telephone us on 01-684 2141 and we will send you details about the Mills & Boon Reader Service Subscription Scheme — you'll soon be able to join us in a wonderful world of Romance.

Please note:– **READERS IN SOUTH AFRICA** write to Mills & Boon Ltd., Postbag X3010, Randburg 2125, S. Africa.

---

Please send me details of the Mills & Boon Reader Service Subscription Scheme.

NAME (Mrs/Miss) _____ EP6

ADDRESS _____

_____

COUNTY/COUNTRY _____

POSTCODE _____

BLOCK LETTERS PLEASE